Copyright © 2020 by Tammy Andresen

All rights reserved.

No part of this book may be reproduced in any form or by any electronic or mechanical means, including information storage and retrieval systems, without written permission from the author, except for the use of brief quotations in a book review.

❦ Created with Vellum

Keep up with all the latest news, sales, freebies, and releases by joining my newsletter!

www.tammyandresen.com

Hugs!

CHAPTER ONE

Lord Callum Exmouth stood on the edge of the large ballroom, strategically near one of the open garden doors. The spring breeze kept the air around him fresh and made him feel less trapped by the crowd. Large social gatherings made him uncomfortable. Not that he couldn't participate in them, he just didn't like them.

He rolled his neck from side to side, causing it to crack. Hell, he hated parties and balls. Unlike the other men in his circle, he hadn't grown up knowing he was part of the peerage. His friends called him Exile, and the name suited him. He was an outcast, especially among his own family.

A gentleman bumped him and Exile let out a deep rumble of dissatisfaction. The man looked over at him, his brow scrunched until he caught Exile's gaze then his own eyes widened in surprise. "I beg your pardon." The man shuffled off quickly giving several worried glances backward.

He cracked two of his knuckles as if to underscore his point. Exile had that effect on people. His sheer size was intimidating.

Exile's cousin, Ewan, was supposed to be the next Earl of Exmouth. Ewan had been born and raised for the position of a Scottish earl and had taken to the role naturally. Fair and decent, Ewan would have made an excellent leader of his people. Exile thought back to his larger-than-life cousin. Though, physically speaking, they'd been the same size, even as kids, Ewan had always known what to do. One summer, Exile had stayed with his aunt and uncle on their estate north of Glasgow. While playing with a group of boys, one of them had fallen from a tree and broken his arm. At twelve years of age, Ewan had taken charge. He'd sent one child for help, another was to hold the boy's hand, a third was to go directly to the doctor. At ten, Exile had wondered if he'd ever be as capable as Ewan. Now at eight and twenty he was still asking himself that same question.

Two ladies passed by him, gossiping loudly. "Did you see the cut of her dress? Awful."

"I know," the other replied, snapping open her fan and giving him a long stare over the top.

Exile looked away, not interested. His mind was elsewhere in the past. More and more he thought of his cousin rather than less. Ewan should be the earl now. Instead, Ewan had died five years prior. The worst part was his cousin had left this world attempting, as usual, to do the right thing. Exile's gut clenched. Bloody unfair. So now, his family, his people, were stuck with Exile as their earl. No one was happy about it. Certainly not his aunt. Definitely not the farmers who grumbled about how much time he spent in England and most certainly not himself.

Exile had never wanted the responsibility. Of course, he still tried to do the best he could. Hell, he'd even gone into business running a gaming hell to make sure his people remained fed. Not that anyone would appreciate his efforts if they knew the truth. They'd likely call him morally corrupt. On several occasions his aunt had outright told him he wasn't the man Ewan had been. She wasn't wrong. In fact, Exile mostly agreed.

He shifted, uncomfortable with where his thoughts had dragged him. A woman with a large feathered hat stepped in front of him, the plumes reaching several feet in the air and blocking his view. As he moved, he caught sight of the door. His friend and fellow club owner walked into the room. The Duke of Darlington, being a full head taller than everyone else, was easy to spot. Next to him was his wife, Minnie. Her bright red hair also standing out in the crowd. He searched just behind her and saw the woman he'd originally come to see: Lady Diana Chase.

His insides tightened. He hadn't meant to react like that. He'd gone to the ball to see her, yes, but not to be with her. In fact, he already had an intended, though he hadn't chosen that woman either. Fiona was Ewan's fiancée and his aunt was convinced that Exile should honor the commitment. If he recalled, her exact words were to the effect of, "It's the least you could do."

His chest puffed out as he drew in a long breath. Marry a woman he'd never even met? Then again, after all the losses his aunt had endured, he wasn't certain how he could refuse.

He gazed across the room at Diana, his body clenching with awareness. He'd met her a month ago when she and her sisters had arrived at the illicit club in the middle of the night. Diana's sister, Emily, had been in search of her fiancé. But the ladies had put both their reputations and the club's secret nature at risk by going there. Even worse, one of

Darlington's enemies knew the ladies had been there.

As a result, Exile and his friends had agreed to keep watch over the Chase women. Make sure they didn't expose their secret or run into trouble themselves. A promise Exile couldn't regret more. Every time he looked at Diana, his breath froze in his chest like a bloody schoolboy with his first crush.

Darlington caught sight of Exile and headed straight for him. Inside Exile swore a string of curses. He should have refused to come here tonight. He should have stayed home. But he'd made a promise and the stakes of that promise had gotten more serious the past few days.

"You came," Darlington rumbled as he reached out his hand to shake Exile's.

Exile gave a single nod, making certain not to look at Diana. "Aye. I came."

"I suppose you're both worried after the incident with Cordelia…." Diana spoke from his left.

He still didn't look at her but that didn't stop her voice from vibrating through him. It was stronger and more confident than many women but beautifully musical with high, rich tones. The sound struck a chord deep inside him.

He turned toward her then, his heart stopping as he looked into those deep, dark brown eyes, fringed with long, black lashes. She was tall for a woman, allowing him to really drink in the details of her face as he himself was well over six feet. Her straight nose was punctuated by the tiniest upturn at the end, her full lips begged to be kissed, her high cheekbones only accentuating that fact.

Diana's dark hair was piled atop her head in a soft coif that made him long to touch the strands and he gripped his thigh to keep his hand in place. "Can't be too careful," he murmured, still drinking in every detail. Her dress came well off the shoulder, exposing her delicate skin and showing her cleavage. He'd like to kiss a path down her neck and over her shoulder, cutting across her chest and—

"With the Countess of Abernath loose about London, we must be very careful when we're out in public," Darlington spoke in a low voice, bending his head so as not to be overheard. He likely needn't have bothered, the room was so loud, Exile could barely hear himself think.

"Let's step outside. We'll be able to hear each other out there." Minnie wrapped her arm through her husband's and they both moved toward the open doors.

Exile had no choice but to hold out his elbow to Diana. As her delicate fingers slipped into his elbow, he flexed the muscles in his arm attempting to curb his reaction to her touch. "Did Cordelia and Malice successfully leave for Dover?"

Diana nodded. "They did. Cordelia seemed very relieved to have left London after what the countess did."

Exile grimaced. Darlington's former fiancée, the Countess of Abernath, had stolen Cordelia from her own home. She'd been attempting to blackmail Cordelia into exposing the club and Darlington's involvement. "Can't say that I blame her. I'm surprised ye've come out at all."

Diana shrugged. "Ada and Grace are at home. But we need to make public appearances or society will begin to wonder what's happened to us and I'm most suited to stand in for the family."

His shoulders straightened as he stared at her, admiration filling his chest. "Ye are a verra strong lass."

She looked up at him then, a small smile curving her lips. "I'll take that as a compliment. Thank you."

"I meant it as a compliment. Ye're welcome." She was just the sort of woman a Scottish man would like to walk beside. Strong, beautiful, ready to speak her mind and fight for the ones she loved.

And she could never be his.

———

DIANA GAVE the large Scot next to her a sidelong glance. The man was interesting, she'd give him that. He was large, not fat, but tall and thickly muscled. He had broad features that would never work for a woman but looked handsome on a man. His square jaw and heavily corded neck gave him an air of power and physical presence.

He was the sort of man a weaker woman might want to hide behind. Diana didn't hide from anything.

"The question, now that we've decided I'm of strong stock, is what does a man do with such a dominant woman?" She wasn't sure why she asked except that most men were a bit afraid of her. But not him. He looked right at her. In fact, his gaze was so strong, she often found herself shifting uncomfortably.

Exile swallowed, his Adam's apple bobbing. Then he mumbled so softly she almost didn't hear him, "I can think of a thing or two."

She nearly tripped over her own feet. She'd known that he was attracted to her from their first meeting. When they were together, his eyes never left her. But men often were enamored with her beauty until they got to know her better.

One man had made her believe he'd liked her just the way she was, but he turned out to be a liar on so many levels. She supposed she should give Exile a few points for honesty, but his innuendo reminded her that she wasn't dealing with a gentleman. Exile, just like the cad in her past, Charles Crusher, was a rogue. And once a rogue, always a rogue.

"Can you now?" she asked, stopping. Minnie and Darlington were just ahead. "Such a gentleman."

He grimaced, coming to a stop as well. "My apologies," He turned toward her. "I didna mean to offend."

His brogue tickled her ears, sliding down her neck. "You're not the first to make such insinuations and you won't be the last." She turned forward to begin walking again. "I don't pay any of you any mind."

He held her in place, not moving. "I'm just like those other men, am I?" His voice had dropped deeper, lower, almost sinister. "Would those other men follow ye from ball to ball to keep you safe?"

Diana raised her brows, giving him a long look. Why did part of her like this protective behavior? "Is that what you're doing?"

He shrugged. "Perhaps."

Diana gave her head a shake. "If that is, in fact, your real motive, I don't need you to follow me about, Lord Exmouth. Continue with your life and leave me to mine."

"I can't." His other hand came to her waist. Tingling heat spread through her at the touch. "I've made a promise and though I'm not as good a man as I'd like to be, I do keep my word."

What did that mean? He wasn't as good a man as he wanted to be? "I'm sure you do. I pride myself on needing no one's help."

He gave his head a shake. "Forgive me for stating the obvious but a lady doesn't have much choice in the matter."

"I have choices," she answered, notching up her chin. Unlike many women, she had money of her own that her mother and father had set aside for her. Perhaps she'd travel the world or open a bookstore. It didn't matter as long she wasn't subverted to someone else's will. "Enough of them, anyhow."

"Do tell," he answered. Darlington and Minnie had stopped just ahead and turned back to look at them.

"You're falling behind," Minnie called. "Shall we stay here and chat or should we walk a bit? I find I don't wish to go back to the party just yet."

"Let's walk," Exile answered.

Diana prickled, her spine snapping straighter. She didn't need him to talk for her. "I think—" She started but suddenly she lurched to the side as he gave her a push. Exile then grabbed her waist and righted her, but Minnie and Darlington had already begun walking. She stopped, stomping her slipper on the stone path. "You did that on purpose."

"Guilty," he answered. "We're not done talking."

"I say we are done," she hissed back.

"Do ye think ye'll marry?" he asked, ignoring her completely.

The man was thick. Not physically, well technically he was very well-muscled, but at this moment she meant mentally. And why was he prodding like this? It was a raw subject for her. "It's none of your business, but I doubt it very much."

His hand at her waist tightened and he drew her closer. "Ye…unmarried?"

Her breath caught as his heat began to seep in through her dress. She tsked, looking up at him. "You don't know anything about me."

"I ken a few things," he said, dropping his face closer to hers. "I ken yer blood sings with passion. I can feel it even now."

She opened her mouth to answer but no words came out. He was right, of course, and her passionate nature had gotten her into a fair bit of trouble already. "You're wrong."

"I'm not." His mouth dropped even closer to hers. "I can prove it too."

"How?" Had she just asked that out loud? Why

had she done that? But she already knew. She was attracted to him, the rapid beat of her heart affirmed that fact with every thump. And part of her, the very bad part, wanted what he was about to do.

By way of answer, he dropped his mouth to hers, his lips pressing hers closed. Fire and heat, and sweet, stinging passion shot through her veins, making her gasp in delight. He lifted his mouth again but only for a moment before he kissed her again and then a third time, each building the tension in her body until she wanted to crush herself against that large chest.

What had she just done?

CHAPTER TWO

Exile lifted his head, looking down into Diana's dark, half-lidded eyes. Bloody Christ, there had been more passion in those small kisses than entire nights he'd spent with other women. He wasn't comparing, there was no comparison. Something about her scent, like fresh snow, and her taste, a hint of peppermint, and the feel of her lips, so soft and so eager. His body vibrated with untapped passion.

Then he cursed, silently at least. He wasn't supposed to want this woman. Would resisting Diana be easier or harder if his fiancée wasn't some faceless lady with only a name? Fiona MacFarland was some laird's daughter who'd been promised to Ewan since childhood. All he could see right now was the woman in front of him, her plump lips parted as though she were waiting for another kiss.

Damn, he wanted to give one to her.

"So, have I proven my point?" The moment the words left his mouth, he wished he hadn't said them.

For a moment, her eyes clouded with confusion, then she snapped back and away from him. The loss of her soft body pressed against his filled him with regret and he longed to pull her close again. But he'd spoken those words for a reason. They needed distance between them. He should have never kissed her in the first place. He just hadn't been able to help himself.

"You've made several points," she said, her voice taking on a sharp edge that cut as deeply as any knife.

He winced. "I'm sorry, lass. I should not have done it. A man better than myself would never take advantage of an innocent woman and I—"

"Enough." She let go of his arm and began walking away from him. Lifting her skirts, she picked up the pace, clearly intent upon catching Minnie. "You assume too much."

"What does that mean?" he asked starting after her. "What do I assume?"

She huffed, lifting her skirts high enough that he got a view of her ankles, very slender, lovely little things that tapered off into silk slippers. "I don't want or need your apology. I am a woman who made a choice to kiss you."

He reached her side and rather pointedly slipped an arm about her waist. "Did ye now?" The way he remembered it, she'd refused to acknowledge there was something between them and he'd been proving a point. Honestly, she was rather fixated on being in charge of her own destiny. Was she just the strong sister of the Chase girls?

"I did," she huffed, trying to slip from his embrace.

"And if I stopped and tried to kiss you again?"

She hit him with her hand square in the stomach. Clearly he had a soft spot. He let out a soft whoosh of breath. "Then I shall tell the Duke of Darlington."

His head snapped back and he arched a brow because she had him there. "But ye don't want to marry me either. Ye've said so."

She let out a harrumph. "Might be worth it, just to prove my point."

He couldn't help it, he laughed. "Ye're a prickly one."

"I am." She held her chin higher. "Bossy too. Loud, opinionated. I've even been called brash." Her skirts swished as they continued to walk. "You might find me beautiful now but just wait."

He pressed his lips together as he gave her a

pointed look. She was convinced that her personality would deter him. The truth was, he liked her just the way she was. "If you ask me, ye're pretty near perfect. Yer problem isna that ye're too much of anything. Ye're just English."

She spluttered then, twisting toward him and grabbing his arm. "You don't like that I'm English?"

"I dinnae care either way." He smiled, knowing that he confused her, but he honestly found this conversation more amusing by the second. She was bloody fun when she was annoyed. "My mother was English and it's her family home that I live in now."

"Then what did you mean?"

Her little foot stomped again. She had a temper to be certain. He'd like to kiss that foot and then the ankle he'd caught a glimpse of. He wanted to kiss higher still, over her calf and…his cock jumped again. Gritting his teeth, he answered her question. "Just that the English seem to want women with no personality at all. Any Scot would jump at the chance to be with a woman of such high…spirit as yerself."

"Oh." She slumped, her fingers pressing to her cheek. "That was actually a lovely compliment and I—"

"There you two are," Darlington called, emerging from the darkness just ahead. "We should go back inside. We're here to be seen and so let's be seen and be done with it. As you ladies know, we need to speak with Jack about why he and Emily eloped. We're meeting them in a few hours' time."

Exile grimaced. Partly because he didn't want to end their garden chat. But also because he wasn't looking forward to the conversation with Jack, who had been engaged to Diana's sister, Emily, when the two had unexpectedly eloped. That decision had sent all of them, men and women alike, spinning into quite the mess and this conversation was sure to be a difficult one.

"Don't be too hard on him." Minnie reached for her husband's arm. "He's sure to have a good reason."

"He'd better," Daring replied.

Exile agreed.

Diana stood in the ballroom watching the dancers spin about. Tonight was odd, indeed. Normally she'd be out there with the rest of the ladies, but tonight she was content to partially hide behind Lord Exmouth.

She supposed she was unsettled by the events of the past few weeks. Cordelia's abduction, Emily's elopement, and her own broken heart had left her feeling exposed and vulnerable.

Then, of course, there was the fact that she'd allowed Lord Exmouth to kiss her. Why had she done that? Hadn't she learned her lesson already?

Many men found her intimidating, but last winter she'd met one who seemed to enjoy her for who she was. Much like Exmouth, Charles Crusher had looked her in the eye and kept looking. Then he'd pursued her. Relentlessly. Every party, he found an invitation. Every calling hour, he'd been there. Even in the driving rain, he'd come to visit. They'd gone for sleigh rides in the snow, and long winter walks, wrapped together under the winter sun.

He'd found opportunities to pull her from the paths and steal kisses when her chaperones weren't looking.

Much like Exmouth had tonight. Her breath caught. How had she allowed another man to take such liberties? Apparently, for all her strength, she was a plain fool when it came to handsome and determined men.

She took another step back and surveyed Lord Exmouth. His hair was longer than most and pulled back into a queue. Rather unconventional and her first clue he was up to no good. Only pirates and thieves wore their hair like that, not earls. Large, broad shoulders tapered down to a thin waist and, heaven help her, a muscular rear that only accented his powerful thighs. Why were a man's thighs tempting? She wasn't certain but a sudden vision of her legs wrapped about his made her flush with heat.

"I feel ye staring at me," he said not turning around to look at her.

She sniffed. "Please. Don't be ridiculous."

He turned his head to the side so she could see the slight smile that curved his lips in profile. "Should we take another walk?"

"No!" she said too quickly and far too loudly. Then she smoothed her skirts. "I've already told you, you needn't be here at all."

"Then why stare?" His eyes brows rose as he continued pivoting toward her.

She straightened her shoulders. She'd never tell him that she'd been contemplating the feel of his body against hers. Such nonsense would only encourage him. "Trying to figure out how I'm going to get rid of you."

He laughed then, deep and rich, and her own cheeks flushed. She liked that he didn't get fussed about her barbs. That he was strong and confident enough to laugh at them. "Touché."

She stepped next to him then. "How much longer does His Grace think we should stay?"

"Not too long. We're meeting at the club in an hour."

Her insides fluttered at the reminder. Jack was going to explain why he and Emily had eloped. And Diana had every intention of speaking with her sister as well. "Can I ask you a favor?"

"O'course," he answered.

"Will you tell me what Jack says?" She looked over to him.

He grimaced and then shook his head. "I dinnae think that's wise."

Stepping closer, she looked over to where Minnie and Daring stood with their heads bent together. Thank goodness her cousin was newly married. Her mother allowed the couple to chaperone but they were so wrapped in one another they barely paid attention. "I'll tell you what Emily shares with us tonight."

He straightened. "What happened between them is no' my concern."

She cocked her head to one side. "They've called you all together. What if what happened jeopardized the club?"

He swore under his breath. She thought it might be Gaelic. "Ye've got a point there, lass."

Moving a bit closer, she dropped her voice. "I knew the countess would do something awful.

Though I never imagined that she would steal away my sister. Mark my words, she isn't done. If we're going to fight her, we must first understand her."

He narrowed his gaze. "Are ye making plans?"

She pressed her lips together. The truth was…she was. The countess seemed to target the women who were still single. Neither Grace nor Ada were as strong as Diana. They also had spotless reputations and excellent prospects for marriage, unlike herself. "No plans. I just want to be prepared in case she tries to take my cousin or my sister."

"Or ye," Exmouth said, his voice dropping low. "Which is why ye won't shake me no matter how hard ye try."

One of her hands cocked on her hip. "So to be clear. You won't share information with me nor will you leave me be. You're just going to buzz around me like a common fly?"

"What's that now?" Darlington asked, coming up behind them. "Is Diana insulting you?"

Exmouth straightened. "O' course no'. She's the picture of feminine decorum."

She nearly laughed out loud but managed to keep it in. Those were words that weren't used about her ever.

"Good." Darlington stepped up next to her. "I

think we've been seen enough for one night. Let's go, shall we?"

Diana frowned. If Exmouth wasn't going to share, how would she find out what transpired during that meeting?

CHAPTER THREE

Exile sat in the dimly lit back room of the Den of Sins. The gaming hell he ran with his friends had become like a second home to him over the past few years. Its smoke covered walls a place of comradery and laughter. But not tonight. All five men stared at each other, the tension so thick, he could have cut it with the Celtic short sword strapped to his hip.

A bottle of scotch sat in the center and glasses were in front of each man, but no one drank. The crystal tumblers remained empty.

Each of the men had a nickname that was used only at the club. The Duke of Darlington sat just to his right; Daring, they called him. The man had gotten married recently and hadn't been in the club since. Daring fingered his glass but didn't reach for the scotch. "Why are we here, Effing? Why don't you tell us why you ran off?"

Lord Jackson Effington looked about the room. "I think the other men need some backstory first."

Daring gave a terse nod, his chin taut with tension. "As many of you know, Lady Abernath, my former fiancée, kidnapped Malice's new wife, Cordelia, in an attempt to punish me on Countess Abernath's part. She wants me outed as the owner of this club and my reputation as an upstanding duke tarnished. Apparently, Lady Abernath is willing to go to almost any length to see her goal accomplished."

The men grumbled around him, but Exile remained silent. He knew all of this already. He also understood that Lady Abernath hadn't done the deed herself, instead she'd hired her lover, Lord McKenzie, to steal Cordelia from her home. Exile had delivered McKenzie to a boat and made sure the man had sailed for France. He'd wondered several times if he shouldn't have sunk McKenzie to the bottom of the Thames instead. Ewan had died attempting to show mercy to a man who'd been a horse thief. The man had repaid that kindness with a blade to the side. "The countess is clearly willing to go to lengths we are no'," he said, just loud enough for everyone to hear. "Unless we fight harder, she'll win."

Bad grimaced. "I know you're right, but it's bloody hard fighting a woman."

Strong women were difficult to fight, indeed.

He closed his eyes as the image of Diana danced before him. Damn, the woman had felt bloody amazing in his arms tonight. And she sounded just as good. She had a warrior's spirit. He spread his hands out on the table in front of him. Perhaps he should consider sharing the events of this meeting with her. She might be a great help. Then again, they would be together enough without adding secret meetings of sharing information to the list of times he'd spent in her company. The woman was tempting enough. And he had to resist her in order to honor his cousin's sacrifice. Even now, guilt stabbed behind his breastbone.

"Where is Lady Abernath now?" Vice, the Viscount of Viceroy, asked, leaning forward and snatching the scotch. He poured himself a healthy glass.

"We don't know." Daring ran his hand through his hair then cleared his throat. "When we rescued Cordelia, a fire broke out and Lady Abernath escaped in the chaos."

Exile knew all of this but it still made his

stomach churn. "Is there anything else we should ken before Jack begins?"

Daring hung his head. "When Malice was leaving, he rescued a small boy. It turns out that boy is Lady Abernath's child." His head shook back and forth and he clasped his hands in front of him. "What's worse is, because of his age, there is a possibility he could be mine."

Vice sucked in his breath. "Does Minnie know?"

Daring drew back, his face ashen. "Not yet. I don't want to upset my wife if it isn't true. The child looks nothing like me. I…" His voice tapered off.

Jack spread his hands on the table in front of him. "He could be Lord Abernath's son. She married the man a month after you ended it with her. That tells me they were likely already involved."

"I agree." Daring nodded. "And Abernath did claim the boy already, so even if we learn he isn't Abernath's child, publicly, we never share. Lord Abernath died last month. The little boy, Harry, is already the new earl."

The men nodded in understanding. Exile relaxed a bit. Daring was using his head at least. "It's best for Harry if there's no scandal about his name."

Daring cleared his throat. "But I also know there was a third man she was sharing her bed with. The reason I ended the relationship was because I caught them together. I never learned who the man was, but I know it wasn't Abernath."

The room went silent. Not a chair scraped, not a glass clinked against the table. Finally Jack swallowed. "That's what I wanted to say to you first, Daring." Jack held out his hands in front of him. "The man you caught her with was me."

Daring stood suddenly, his chair flying back against the wall. Exile stood too, worried he might need to intercede between the two men. The last time he'd engaged in a brawl, his cousin had died. His insides pitched but he held his ground.

Daring leaned his fists on the table. "We've been friends for four years and you're just telling me this now?"

"I didn't know you then." Jack remained seated, his hands out. "At the time the affair happened, I had no idea she was involved with anyone else. I thought we were in love. I thought we'd marry." Jack closed his eyes. "I didn't know she was engaged. Hell, no one did. For all we know she was engaged to you and Abernath at the same time." He scrubbed his face. "She cleaned out what little money I had. Emptied my coffers and left me with a mountain of debt." Then he drew in a long breath. "But that isn't all of it. I know for certain that she was also involved with Lord Pennington when she was with me. The day after I ended it, I found them walking in the park together and followed them until I saw..." Jack stopped, his head dropping as he pressed the palms of his hands to his eyes.

Daring slumped over, as though that name took all wind from his sails. "Jesus, Joseph, and Mary. Harry looks just like Pennington."

"He does," Jack answered. "I noticed it the moment I saw him." He leaned closer. "And I'm sorry I didn't tell you. I didn't put it all together until recently and then I wasn't sure if it was wise to tell you what I'd learned. We were already friends. Hell, we'd started a business together. You'd moved on with your life and I thought it might hurt you more to know."

Daring looked down at the table for so long, the men began to shift in their chairs. Finally, he looked up. "The honest truth is catching you in bed with her saved my life." His fists wrapped on the tabletop. "You should have told me. But I do believe she managed to hurt you worse than she did me. She really cleaned you out?"

Jack nodded. "It's why I came to you to start the club in the first place."

Daring scrubbed his face. "We've got a much larger problem now. The women who have been dutifully keeping our secret are in danger. You've each agreed to keep one safe. You're going to have to double your efforts."

Exile drew in a long breath. Diana rose in his thoughts. What had started as a simple task had already begun to feel complicated, his attraction to her the largest of them all. "Circumstances have changed since we first made that agreement. Originally we were just supposed to make sure the ladies didn't share our secret. Now we're trying to protect them from a woman who's unhinged."

"The Chase women have proved more than loyal and Lady Abernath is insane." Daring looked around the table. "You're right, Exile. It's a difficult task to be certain."

"I don't give a bloody bullocks about the task. What's the story with all of you marrying?" Vice took a long swig of his drink. "Makes a man damn nervous."

Exile looked down at the man who appeared to be an angel but was devilish to be certain. "We'll all have to marry eventually."

"Not you too," Vice sneered. "Are you thinking about offering for that dark-haired beauty, Diana?"

"No," he bit out, crossing his arms over his chest. But excitement zinged through his veins just thinking about her. Bloody hell, that did make things complicated.

Diana sat between Minnie and her sister, Grace.

"What do you think they're discussing?" Emily wrung her hands together. "I've got a bad feeling about this. Jack has been so worried and that makes me anxious for him."

Diana cleared her throat. Emily had always been the most nervous of the Chase girls. "I appreciate your concern, Em. But I think you owe us an explanation before we delve into what's happening with Jack." Emily and Jack's relationship had been filled with bumps.

Ada poked Diana in the back, whispering in her ear, "Be nice."

Diana let out a long breath. "I am being nice." Wasn't anyone going to call Emily out on the fact that she and Jack had eloped with barely a word, leaving them all very worried?

Emily stopped pacing, her face twisting in pain. "I'm sorry for that. When we were at the family party, I got a surprise visit from Lady Abernath."

The girls all sucked in her breath. Grace clutched Diana's hand. "Did she try to steal you away?"

Emily shook her head. "Cordelia gets that honor. But she did threaten me. Said that if I didn't expose

Daring, she would tell the world about Jack and his club. She also said…" Emily flushed a bright red.

"What?" Minnie asked, standing to cross to Emily, then wrapping her arms about her. Diana frowned.

A tear slid down Emily's cheek. "She somehow discovered that I was pregnant with Jack's child. She threatened to expose the baby as a bastard. I know Jack would have married me anyway but we were worried Mum and Dad might cancel the wedding after they learned about Jack's club."

Diana stood, any irritation with Emily burning away at the fire in her belly over what Lady Abernath had done. "So you ran away before Mum and Dad could stop the wedding?"

Emily nodded. "Even if she ruined Jack, at least we'd be wed and the baby would be safe."

Emily shook her head. "She knows something about Jack. Something that could send him to prison. We married and we transferred much of his funds into my name, anything not entailed, which is most of it because of the club." She swallowed. "If Lady Abernath does strike against him, he wanted both me and the baby provided for."

Diana stepped to Emily's other side, her hand touching Emily's arm. "So you ran before she had a chance to strike and you've returned now that he's secured your future."

Emily nodded, her hand rubbing her stomach. "I didn't mean to make you all worry. I'm sorry. We just wanted to protect our child."

Cordelia stepped in front of them, wrapping her arms about everyone. "Of course you did the right thing. Your child comes first."

"Do you know what Jack wanted to discuss with all of them?" Ada asked, joining the hug.

Emily nodded. "I have an idea. Jack had an affair with Lady Abernath years ago."

Minnie gasped. "Does Daring know that?"

Emily shook her head. "He's wanted to tell Daring for years, but he's afraid of the consequences. I love Jack, but his past is full of dark twists and turns and he isn't always open about them."

Ada gave a bright smile. "If anyone can help him to see straight, it's you."

Emily's shoulders slumped. "I feel as though we should help him now. I'm worried how Daring will react to the news."

Minnie winced. "Tag can have a temper. Perhaps the married among us should go to the club and intercede. Make sure the men don't kill each other."

Diana straightened. This was her chance to listen in. "I'm coming too."

"You are not," Minnie shook her head. "Your mother will never forgive us if you're ruined."

Diana made a face. She didn't dare tell her sisters that her fall had already come to pass. Or that she may as well be the one to face Abernath because she had the darkest future of all the Chase women. Her chest ached. She'd miss having a child of her own but she'd do whatever was necessary to keep her sisters safe. "I'm unlikely to marry so it's of no consequence." She waved her hand. "I doubt any of you will be able to stop me, anyhow."

"You are too much, Diana." Cordelia shook her head.

Her head dipped in shame. Cordelia wasn't wrong. She'd done a lot of things that had been too much and gone too far. It's the main reason she wouldn't marry. She doubted any man wanted her strong personality or her mistakes.

"Why do you say you won't marry?" Minnie narrowed her gaze.

Diana shrugged. She wouldn't burden any of them with her sins. "You know better than anyone how off-putting a strong woman is."

Minnie frowned. "That doesn't mean there isn't a man for you."

Diana didn't want to argue the point. How did she tell her cousin that she'd allowed a known rogue to ruin her? "We should go before we're too late. They could have murdered Jack already."

"What?" Emily gasped, tugging on Minnie's arm. "Let's go."

Diana fell in step behind Minnie and Cordelia. If only maneuvering Lady Abernath were so easy.

She drew in a deep breath. Where the countess was concerned, Diana needed a plan.

CHAPTER FOUR

"A toast to Jack's marriage," Vice called, raising his glass in the air. They all swallowed down their snifters of scotch. "May he be happier in the institution than I ever could."

Exile sat with his empty glass in hand, his mind delightfully fuzzy. Dimly, he knew that they hadn't actually accomplished much in terms of the countess. No plan had been made. But they had their friend Jack back and secrets had been revealed, ones that might have really damaged their group. But the men had weathered the storm.

Honestly, Exile thought Jack had been right to keep his affair with the countess quiet. Daring was now happily married. If Jack had shared this tidbit even a year ago, he might have fractured their whole friendship.

Exile raised his glass again. "Let's drink to friendship!"

"To friendship," the men called, all lifting their cups and toasting.

Daring slammed down his cup. "What are we to do about our shared problem?" He peered over at Jack, his head swaying a bit.

Exile stared at his cup. How many snifters had they drunk and why was the glass moving? Wasn't it flat on the table? "What problem?" Had he just slurred? Was Daring discussing how Diana heated his blood even though he was engaged to another woman?

Daring reached for the bottle but seemed to miss. He stared at it for several seconds as he made another grab. "You know. The woman I was once engaged to, who is now stealing our women and threatening our…," he tapered off, then squinting his eyes, looked at Exile. "What was I saying?"

Exile blinked, trying to remember.

"Well isn't this a delightful scene?" a woman called from the door. Did she sound angry? Exile wasn't certain, but then again, why should he care?

But Daring surged to his feet, then promptly sat down, his hands holding his head. "Minnie. I can explain."

"I don't require an explanation." The statuesque,

red-haired woman entered the room, head high. "Here I was thinking you might need my assistance and you're falling-down drunk."

Daring blinked. "I'm not." Then he tried to stand again, pushing off the table and sliding sideways. "Maybe a bit."

She huffed. "This is what I came out for?"

Another voice called from just behind her. "Don't fret, Minnie. It won't be the last time you peel your drunk husband from a chair."

Diana. He knew that voice anywhere. He twisted about to have a look at her and then the entire room began to spin. "Ye came," he slurred, slowly pushing out of his seat. "Were ye worried about me too?"

Vice harrumphed from the chair next to him. "Bloody idiot, it's not too late for you. Run now while you have the chance."

"Oh no, don't run." Diana crossed over to him, placing an arm about him to steady him. "I came just for you and I'm going to see you home, my lord."

Well, wasn't this a delightful surprise? "Where's Diana and what have you done with her?"

Feminine laughter filled the room as Minnie and Emily covered their mouths to hide their mirth. "He's got you there, Diana," Emily called as she helped Jack up.

Minnie clucked her tongue. "You can't see him home. I have to see *you* home."

"Don't be ridiculous. His Grace won't survive the carriage ride. You need to get him straight back to your house."

"But…" Minnie straightened. "I'll leave him here."

Diana tried not to curse but a small, "Damn," slipped from her lips. She wanted to use the ride to extract some information from a very drunk man.

Minnie's eyebrows rose. Emily teetered with a swaying Jack draped across her shoulders. "Are you sure, Diana? You're not worried you'll be ruined?"

"She thinks she won't marry." Minnie huffed but had to grab Daring as he started to topple over. "You swear you'll be all right?"

"I'll be fine." Victory sang in Diana's veins and a little excitement at being left alone with the earl. "In fact, I'll come to your house directly after I've dropped him. Then mother will never be the wiser. You can substantiate my story."

Minnie curled her fingers into fists. "I don't like this plan one bit."

But Daring gave a sick gurgle. "I haven't been drinking much of late. I'm afraid I may have overdone it."

Diana pressed her lips together, hiding a smile, as the man turned rather green. Minnie began pulling him toward the door. "You'd best be sick outside."

Emily followed with Jack.

"Are you ready to be escorted home, my lord?" Diana wrapped her arms tighter about Exile.

He looked down at her, his eyes darkening. She shifted uncomfortably at the same time her blood heated. She shouldn't want him. He was a rogue and this was a fact-finding endeavor. She needed to know exactly what his friends had told him about Lady Abernath.

"I'm ready." His gaze held hers as he stared into her eyes, heat radiating from his body as it pressed to hers.

"I'll come too," Vice stood. "Wouldn't want the lady to be-—"

"No," both her and Exmouth said at the exact same moment.

"Bloody hell," Vice mumbled, looking over at Bad.

Diana tore her gaze from Exile to consider the baron. He didn't appear the least bit drunk and he'd been quiet since they'd entered. His dark gaze pierced into hers. "Let them go," Bad murmured. "We already know where this will lead."

Diana squinted her eyes. "What does that mean?"

But he waved his hand, dismissing her words.

The man was a bit unsettling and Diana was rarely intimidated by anyone. "You've gotten your wish. Take it." Then he turned to Vice. "Know any lords who might be willing to go into business with us? Our numbers are rapidly dwindling with these Chase women sniffing about."

"I'm not sniffing," she huffed even as she began to steer Exmouth to the door. Much as she'd like to argue, Bad was correct. She shouldn't squander this opportunity. "We'll discuss this again, another time."

"I doubt it," Bad answered and then turned away.

She paused for a moment. Did she demand the man listen? But Exmouth leaned closer, his warm breath tickling her ear. "Are ye ready?"

Her stomach dropped. How did she answer that? While she knew he was asking if Diana was ready to leave, somehow she wanted him to ask for more. Much more.

EXILE STRAIGHTENED a bit the moment they stepped out into the fresh air, it instantly cleared his head.

He glanced down at Diana, her arms wrapped about his middle as she walked him down the dark alley. Her body snug against his in the most satisfying way. Tall and slender, there was still a softness about her that felt…just right.

"Where's your carriage?" she asked, her eyes scanning the alley.

"Douglas called for it, it'll be here in just a moment." Then he wrapped another arm about her. "Are ye cold, lass? I'll warm ye."

"No, I…" She stopped, searching the darkness again. "What was that?"

He peered into the night, blinking, then he scrubbed his face. Why had he had so much to drink. "I don't see…" But his voice fell away. There was in fact a movement in the shadow. He gripped Diana tighter with one arm even as his other hand grabbed the short sword at his side and pulled the sharp metal blade from its sheath. "Who goes there?"

Diana sucked in her breath, her arms tightening about his middle.

A figure lunged from the darkness, making a grab for them but in a second, Exile reacted. He pushed Diana behind him and slashed with his blade. The man lunged away but not in time and Exile felt the tip of his sword rip through clothing.

"Ahhhhh," a man yelled, wincing away.

Exile started after him even as the man ducked and spun.

"My lord," Diana cried, a choking sound clogging

her voice as she grabbed for his back. "Don't leave me."

He stopped, watching the man skulk away, slightly bent, one shoulder stooped lower than the other. Part of him wanted to chase after the man and sink his blade through his ribs. The last time he'd been attacked like that, Ewan had ended up dead. The blade had been meant for Exile but it had found his cousin instead. "I would never leave ye, lass. Dinnae ye worry about that."

"I..." she whimpered. "I shouldn't have come tonight."

"No, ye shouldn't have but no' because of that pile of shite. I would never let anyone hurt ye." He meant every word. The fight had sharpened his mind and as he looked down at her, her arms about her waist, a surge of protectiveness like he'd never felt before coursed through him. He'd protect her with his very last breath. Without thought, he reached out and pulled her close again, folding her into his arms. She pressed against him, her cheek resting against his chest.

"Will you take me to Minnie's please?"

Her voice trembled and he nodded against the top of her head. "Of course." He started rubbing circles along her back. "My carriage will be here any moment."

She nodded against him, the top of her head snuggling into his chin. Her silky hair tickled his neck as her scent wafted into his nostrils. He held her closer, placing a light kiss on the strands. He wanted to hold her like this all night, keep her wrapped in his embrace where she'd be warm and safe. Would she notice if they just stood there, wrapped together?

As if in answer, the rumbling of wheels filled the alley along with the clop of horses' hooves. He recognized his driver, and waving to the man to stay in his seat, he snapped open the door himself and lifted Diana into his arms.

Climbing into the buggy, he snapped the door shut again and then settled onto one of the bench seats, folding Diana onto his lap.

She willingly bent, settling against him. Her derriere was pressed into his lap and he ignored the tightening in his groin, reaching up to stroke her face instead. He brushed his thumb along her eyebrow then swept down over her cheek. "Ye're all right. Ye're safe."

"I know I am," she answered as her face tipping up to his. "Thank you."

"Ye're welcome," he replied looking down at her in the dark interior. Her eyes shone even in the dim light and her lips. Jesus, her lips held a full, soft pout that was so damned tempting.

He wasn't aware of moving, but suddenly their mouths met in a soft kiss that should have been sweeter. Instead, it was full of the sort of passion that made a man ache. The one touch held so much promise that he nearly groaned aloud, just holding the sound in as their eyes met.

She arched her neck again, giving him another kiss and then another until one blended into the next becoming one long joining.

Slanting her lips open, he swiped his tongue along the inside of her mouth, tasting the sweet scent of her, fresh and clean with hints of mint. Diana moaned into his mouth, and in response, he gathered her even closer, deepening their kiss.

Her gloved fingers were wrapped about his neck. But he had the urge to touch her skin, feel its texture underneath his fingertips. Yanking off one of his own gloves, he stroked her neck then trailed his hand down lower until he reached the swell of her breast, still exposed by her evening gown. The smooth, silky plumpness made his thickening cock rock-hard and he cupped her breast outside her gown, wanting more of her.

She arched into the touch and he moved his other hand to the back of her dress. When had he decided to undo the buttons? He didn't care. As the fabric slumped down her front, he reached for her breast again, only a thin layer of silky chemise separating her soft flesh from his hand. Her breasts weren't overly large, but big enough. They filled his palm perfectly, and his hands weren't small. What was more, Diana's nipple puckered under his touch. They both groaned together.

"My lord," she murmured, wiggling in his lap. "I want…"

"What?" His breath held in his lungs as he waited for her answer. What did she want? To make love to him? To have his protection always? To be his wife? In this moment, he might agree to any and all of it, if only she'd take off more of her clothes.

She swallowed and tipped her head back to look at him. "I want to talk to you."

"No," he answered, letting out a groan of frustration. "Anything but that."

Diana blinked up at him. She could feel the evidence of his desire pressing into her backside. With a sigh, she started to sit up. Best to feel less of him if she wanted to actually have this conversation before they arrived at Minnie's home. She was slow to move, though, because honestly, he felt delicious. Strong, hard, and so masculine, his powerful thighs flexed underneath her and near left her breathless and she needed to keep her wits about her. So, pulling herself up she slid backward to remove herself from his lap.

One of his hands, held her hip, giving it a squeeze. It pressed his hardness into her softness and her breath caught. She had the distinct urge to rub against the stiff flesh and test its length, feel the friction. "My—"

"It's Callum," he answered his voice husky.

"Callum." She tested the name in her mouth. Something about the combination of sounds allowed the word to just roll off her tongue. "It suits you."

"Thank ye." He leaned down and captured her lips again. "I dinnae ken that I'll ever have ye half undressed and in my lap again. I intend to take full advantage."

She stiffened away, scrambling from his lap and, nearly falling, managed to toss herself into the seat across from him. Her dress was still undone and she held it up against her chest. "No man is taking advantage of me." She swallowed down a lump of pain. "Not ever again."

He looked across the carriage at her, quiet for a moment before he slowly raised his hand, extending it out to her. "Come here. Ye'll freeze over there."

"I shouldn't." But her body ached to fit against his again. What a traitor it was. Even now, she wanted to feel his touch, the hard press of him. Why? Likely because she was a harlot. Why else did she continue to be attracted to men who didn't want to commit to her even after she'd allowed them liberties?

But he lifted from his seat and reaching for her hand, pulled her across the carriage and settled her back into his lap. Her breath shortened as she looked up at his handsome features, so rugged and yet somehow, comforting. Rather than kiss her, however, he began to rebutton the back of her dress. "I think ye're right. It's time we talked."

Her mouth pressed together. She should jump on this opportunity. Instead, she wanted to burrow against him like a child. Why had her strength abandoned her? "All right."

"Diana, what did ye mean when you said ye won't let a man take advantage of ye ever again? Which man took advantage the first time?"

She sucked in her breath. Had she really said that? "I only meant you."

He wrapped his arms about her back, hugging her to his chest. "Ye did not."

She looked at the window, not that she could see

out. The curtains were firmly drawn. "I had a suitor last year. I thought we'd marry. We didn't."

His arms tightened. "And what liberties did ye allow him?"

She shook her head, still not meeting his eyes. She shouldn't tell him. Diana hadn't even shared the truth with her sisters. But somehow, wrapped in his embrace, she'd never wanted to tell someone more. Share the secret she'd been holding inside. "I allowed him all the liberties a woman can give."

CHAPTER FIVE

Exile closed his mouth to keep the string of curses from falling out. Rage beat at his chest. He didn't know who the man was, but he was going to kill him slowly.

Granted, Exile had also taken liberties. He knew that. But he had a genuine affection for Diana. A little voice in his head argued that the end result was the same. Only not entirely because he and Diana had stopped well before all the liberties had been had. "Who?"

Diana squirmed a bit and he ignored the tightening of his groin. The time for passion was past. "I can't tell you that."

"Minnie will tell me if ye don't," he said, giving her a bit of a squeeze. It was true. If the man had been a suitor then any of the Chase women could identify him.

She gasped then pushed at his chest. "You wouldn't."

"I would," he answered. "Tell me the truth. Why are we in this carriage right now?"

She stopped pushing. "I…" She nibbled at her lip

His chest tightened as he resisted the urge to kiss her again. "I'll make ye a deal," he said. "Ye tell me what I want to know and I shall do the same for ye."

Diana paused, her cheek twitching. Finally she answered. "Charles Crusher."

"That egit?" He knew the man. Yes, he had swagger but no real meat to back all his pomp. "He's not even a lord."

She shook her head. "But he is married to a widowed marchioness. One who is rather wealthy."

Callum growled. "I understand." The man had tossed Diana over when a fatter purse had presented itself.

She shook her head. "Your turn. What did Jack say?"

Callum grimaced. "Well, that he had an affair with Lady Abernath and he was the man that Daring actually caught in bed with our fair countess."

"Oh dear." Diana tapped his shoulder. "That is

sticky but doesn't explain anything about why Lady Abernath is so angry or what she plans."

He nodded. "He also said that Harry was conceived around the time both Daring and Jack were involved with her."

Diana stopped tapping. "So Harry could be Jack or Daring's son?"

Exile winced. He'd agreed to share this information because he'd needed to know that name. Something inside him had to right Diana's wrongs, but he might have just made a terrible mistake. "Ye can't tell them. Promise me ye won't share this information with Minnie or Emily."

Diana let out a long sigh. "You likely should have made me promise that before you told me."

"Woman," he rumbled.

She rolled her eyes. "Don't start. I'll keep yet another secret. It's becoming a habit. But you should know, I'm only staying quiet to give Daring and Jack the opportunity to sort this all out before my family is hurt."

"If it makes ye feel better, Harry's been claimed by Abernath and he's the spitting image of Pennington, her fourth lover of that particular time period."

Diana slumped against him. "That makes me feel much better, actually. And it also explains Lady

Abernath's anger. Both Jack and Darlington left her when she likely felt she needed them."

Exile shook his head. "She was sleeping with four men at once."

Diana wrinkled her nose, frowning. "We can't all be pillars of virtue."

He blinked. Was she comparing what they had just done to what Lady Abernath had? "What just happened between us is completely different."

"How?" she asked sitting up higher to stare into his eyes.

He wasn't sure what to say. It came to mind that he had a real affection for her and yet, the end result was the same. He had a fiancée already. He'd never hated the idea more. "I would never leave ye to fend for yerself if ye were carrying my child."

She quirked a brow. "I see." But her frown didn't relax. "But if I didn't become pregnant, you'd be comfortable ruining me with a physical relationship?"

His mouth opened and then closed. He tried to speak again but no words came out. "That isnae what I meant."

She shook her head. "It doesn't matter. Whether or not Lady Abernath is justified in her anger, I am sure she feels abandoned by the men who left her. I'm beginning to understand her motivation at least."

The carriage rumbled to a stop. Had they reached Daring's house already? "This conversation isnae over." They had so much more they needed to discuss. What had happened between them, and why he couldn't marry her.

She held her face in his hands and placed a soft kiss on his lips. "It definitely is. Good night, my lord."

She'd used his formal address again. No more Callum, rolling off her tongue. Good night had sounded a great deal like goodbye.

———

Diana slumped against the front door of Minnie and Daring's townhouse listening to Callum's carriage roll away. What had she just done?

She dropped her head into her hands. She couldn't believe that she'd allowed another man to kiss her, touch her intimate places. Callum's touch was so much more exciting than Charlie's had ever been. Her first lover had been thrilling in idea. A man not intimidated by her and willing to pursue her relentlessly. But somehow the act had been disappointing. Not just when he'd taken her maidenhead but even the kisses, the touches, they'd been…tolerable.

Callum, however, made her body sing. She drew in a deep breath, vowing never to be alone with the man again. With Charlie, she'd somehow thought by giving herself to him, he'd offer. He'd been pulling away and she'd hated that. Now she knew he'd found a new romantic interest but at the time…

The circumstances were completely different this time around. Callum was not going to offer for her hand. Unless of course, she ended up pregnant. Not that she would. She'd have to take great pains not to end up alone with him again because if she did, she might very well be tempted.

She knew who Callum was. He was the owner of an illicit club, a man who would have to be dragged into matrimony.

Then again, Daring and Jack had succumbed. Even Lord Malicorn had married Cordelia and that man seemed far darker than Callum ever could.

And Callum already knew her secret. The one that had convinced her she'd never be able to marry. How would she explain to her husband that she'd fallen so short of purity?

Callum was attracted to her and protective? Was he her future?

She pushed off the door just as Minnie came down the stairs.

"How's Daring?"

Minnie wrinkled her nose. "Terrible. The big lout."

Diana pressed her lips together to keep from smiling. "Terrible?"

"He's emptied his stomach and then dropped into sleep like a stone sinks to the bottom of the lake." Minnie stopped in front of her. "I expected you to take longer. Did you behave yourself?"

Diana shrugged. "More or less. A man tried to rob us in the back of the club."

Minnie gasped, "What?"

"Don't worry. Callum had the situation well in hand."

Minnie raised her brows. "Callum?"

"Stop repeating one word with a question mark. It's annoying."

"Sorry?" Minnie crossed her arms. "When did Lord Exmouth become Callum?"

Diana rubbed her temples with the tips of her fingers. "About the time he sliced some man with his short sword to protect me."

"Oh." Minnie reached for her hand. "No wonder he brought you straight here."

Diana grimaced as she gave Minnie's fingers a squeeze. The two began to walk up the stairs together. Part of her wanted to tell her cousin what she'd learned about Daring and Lady Abernath but she held her tongue. "Any thoughts on what the countess will do next?"

They reached the top of the stairs and Minnie stopped. "That's an abrupt change of conversation."

Not in her mind. "Apologies. The entire reason I wanted to take Callum home was to learn what Jack had said. I feel if I understand the Countess of Abernath better, I'll know her next plan."

Minnie nodded. "Did you learn anything?"

Diana's insides wriggled with discomfort. "Not much."

Minnie let out a loud sigh. "It's good that we're keeping Ada and Grace out of society. The woman is clearly capable of anything."

Lying to the ones she loved? Being morally corrupt? She gave a shiver as she realized how she herself was a lighter shade of Lady Abernath. "I feel sorry for her."

"What?" Minnie asked as they rounded the corner. She opened a door and gestured for Diana to enter. A maid already waited to help Diana undress.

Diana shrugged. "I know she's deranged but what happened to make her that way? I mean it, Minnie. I feel like we're more alike than everyone wants to acknowledge. She's strong and tough. What would happen if someone took a woman like that and broke her?"

Minnie shook her head. "You're making a few large leaps there. How do you know she isn't just evil?"

Diana sighed. She couldn't prove her theory but she sensed Lady Abernath hurt deep inside. No Diana didn't have four lovers at once, but she had allowed more than one man access to her and she knew the pain that came with being rejected. What if Lady Abernath's past was far darker than hers? "You're right. I have no proof. Just a feeling."

"Ok, so what does your feeling tell you?" The maid began unbuttoning Diana's dress.

"She's growing desperate. Now she's out of her home, her son is gone, nothing has happened to the men she's tried to hurt. Whatever she does next, it will be big and it will strike hard."

"Who?" Minnie's voice had a breathy quality that expressed her fear.

Diana winced. "Honestly, either you, because you are Daring's wife, or me."

"Why you?" Minnie asked clutching her own neck.

"I'm bait. We've tucked Ada and Grace away." At least until the season started in a few short weeks.

Minnie closed her eyes. "Do you have any theories on what she might do?"

Diana bit her lip. The truth was, she did. They'd

gone from verbal threats, to kidnapping. The next logical bridge was physical violence. But how far would she take that, and would she come at them herself? With Cordelia, she'd sent a lover to do the actual snatching. Lady Abernath's most significant quality was her ability to manipulate men. "I have some ideas…" But she didn't want to tell Minnie. Because Minnie would then tuck Diana away with Ada and Grace. "But they're nothing you should be worried about." Lie. It was a complete lie.

CHAPTER SIX

Callum stepped out of his carriage into the dark alley behind the club. After what had happened, he had no intention of going home. Instead, he wanted to look about the area where they'd been attacked and warn the men about the attacker.

The sun would start to rise soon enough but for now, the night still shrouded the city in darkness. He was only able to find a few spots of blood. Whoever the man had been, his coat had received the worst of the blow. Exile unsheathed his short sword. Only the very tip had a staining of red blood. He grimaced. The man had only received a scratch.

Scrubbing his face, he entered the back door of the club using his key. The gaming hell had shut down hours before and the guards had all retired for the night. As he made his way down the hall, however, he realized that Bad and Vice were still here. Their voices floating down to him in the darkness. Then he heard another male's voice, his deep timbre unrecognizable. Drawing his blade again, he stalked down the hall.

The narrow passage opened into their back room. Bad sat with his feet upon the table while Vice casually shuffled cards.

Exile's eyes narrowed. A third man sat next to Vice as though he owned the place. Who the hell was he and why was he back here? "I don't believe we've met," he growled out in his deepest voice.

"Exile." Vice dropped the cards. "You came back. I…I'm surprised."

"Obviously," he answered, still staring at the newcomer. The man was ridiculously handsome, though rather pale. He looked back at Exile with weary eyes, his head cocked to the side. "Who is he and why is he here?"

"He's my second cousin." Vice stood. "And he helped Bad out of a scrape this evening."

That got Exile's attention and he turned to Bad. "What sort of scrape?"

Bad looked Exile up and down. "Why is your short sword drawn?"

"I also had a scrape in the alley. A man attacked me and Diana."

"Fuck," Vice blurted out. "No wonder you're back."

Bad gave a single nod. "Sin here caught a man trying to steal."

"Sin?" Exile turned to the fellow. He didn't like him. Wasn't sure why. Perhaps it was just the other man had encroached into his territory.

The man stood, rather slowly and carefully. "The Earl of Sinclair, at your service." He gave a stiff bow.

"You've given him a nickname in keeping with the rest of us?"

Vice held up his hands. "Hear me out, chap. With Daring, Effing, and Malice all married, we need help. Bad has had to work the floor every evening for the past fortnight at least."

Exile grimaced. That was a good point. "Yes, but no one has sold their share. Ye need to ask the group first before you go inviting new people into our secret. If it still is a secret."

Vice winced, rubbing the back of his neck. "That's fair."

"Worry not." Sin held up his hands. "Your secret is safe with me."

Exile crossed his arms, still holding his short sword. "I've heard that before."

"And so far it's been true." Bad pushed back further in his chair.

Exile pivoted to stare down at Bad. "Perfectly respectable women are being attacked in their own homes and behind our club since learning our secret."

Bad shrugged. "That is not my problem. Sin isn't a woman, he won't need our protection. I, however, could use some help, and we can't stop talking about the Chase women long enough for me to actually ask for it."

Grimacing, Exile dropped his arms. "Ye've a point there. But next time, write a missive first, before inviting in someone new."

Vice cleared his throat. "The attack in the alley. Do you think it had anything to do with our lady enemy?"

A wave of shock coursed through him. Why had he not thought of that? Should he have stayed with Diana? Was she at this very moment in danger? Darlington was likely passed out cold. No man could match a Scot in his drinking. "Bloody hell, I shouldn't have left her."

Bad rolled his eyes. "Come on, then. We'll lock up and check on her. But I was right to bring Sin in. You're six steps from the fucking altar."

"I am," he answered truthfully. "But no' how ye think. Matrimony won't change my involvement in the club." Just thinking about his faraway fiancée made him churn with dread.

"Sure. That's what they all say." Bad set his glass on the table. "Let's go, in the wee hours of morning, to check on the woman you are definitely not marrying."

Sin coughed. Was the new guy laughing at him? He looked over at the man, who was even more pale.

"Are you coming, Sin?" Vice asked. Then he noticed Exile's stare. "He's my family. We can trust him."

But Exile ignored Vice, his eyes narrowing. His distrust of Sin intensifying. "You've a stain on your coat."

Sin looked down, his hand covering the dark spot. "Someone must have spilled their drink on me." Then he cleared his throat. "Much as I'd love to learn the details of what you're discussing, I should take myself off to bed."

Vice narrowed his gaze. "You're going to have to improve your drinking."

Sin gave a nod. "Clearly."

Exile gave the man one last look then decided he was another day's problem. What he needed to do now was make sure that Diana was safe.

Diana woke to a noise, but she'd been so deeply asleep, she couldn't remember what the noise had been.

"My lord," the butler said. Was he just outside her door? "You can't go—"

The door banged open and Diana rose up, blood pumping through her veins even as her head spun with the sudden lurch.

"Diana," Exile's voice boomed through the room.

She swayed again pulling the covers up over the night rail that Minnie had allowed her to borrow. "What is it?" Bad and Vice came skidding in behind him and then the fogginess in her brain cleared completely. "What are they doing in my bedroom?" Yanking the covers from the bed, she wrapped them about her and stood. Being in bed made her feel vulnerable.

Exile looked back at both of them. "Out!" he boomed.

Vice grimaced. "And miss the tongue-thrashing she's about to give you? This is the reason I came."

Bad gave a slow smile. "What he said."

Diana brushed her hair back over her shoulder. She and Minnie had stayed up so late she hadn't bothered to braid it and now it hung down her back in what was likely a tousled mess. "Get out." She started move toward them. "Both of you. Now."

Vice gave her a wicked grin. "You look lovely like that, with your hair down. I can see why Exile is so—"

"If ye dinnae get out, I am going to break open yer skull. Dinnae think I won't." Exile gave Vice a shove.

Bad did something she'd never seen before. Just as he was leaving, he winked. Her mouth dropped open. That was the most expressive he'd ever been. Then both men exited the room and her gaze shifted to Exile. "I was asleep."

"I can see that," he answered, crossing over to her. He reached for her face and cupped her cheek.

"Have you slept?" She narrowed her gaze. Why was he here?

He shook his head. "I'll let ye go back to bed. It's just that Vice mentioned that the attack in the alley might somehow be connected to Lady Abernath and I was suddenly concerned for yer safety."

Diana's brows scrunched together. "I suppose it's possible they are somehow connected, but even if they are, that doesn't explain why you're here."

He looked down at her, his mouth open. "Cordelia was snatched by a man right from yer home."

"Someone she was acquainted with did so during calling hours." Diana appreciated his concern, but honestly, it wasn't necessary. She took his hand from her cheek holding it in her own. She had to confess their skin clasped together felt nice. Very nice. She cleared her throat trying to collect her thoughts. "No one is going to be able to break into my bedroom at the Duke of Darlington's house—"

"I did," he answered suddenly pulling her into his embrace.

She looked up at him. "Exactly. You are well known to me and the duke, which is the only reason you have access to me at all."

"What the bloody hell is going on," Darlington growled from the door. Diana looked up to see Bad and Vice just behind him, both grinning like idiots.

"Are they still drunk?"

Exile looked up at them. "It's seven o'clock in the morning. Of course they are."

"We only just stopped drinking." Vice grinned. "I'll be pickled for hours."

Darlington, looking green, bent over. "You had better tell me why you're in Diana's bedroom, holding her in your arms, or I'm going to have to escort you down the aisle to the altar with my derringer."

"We were attacked in the alley," Diana answered her voice both light and soft. "Lord Exmouth was worried the attack was somehow connected to Lady Abernath and that I was in immediate danger."

Daring lifted his head, his skin an alarming shade of green. "Why wasn't I notified of the attack?"

Minnie squeezed past Bad and Vice, her hair down, clad in a dressing gown. "Because you were out cold, you big blockhead."

Vice snorted a laugh while Bad chuckled. "The ladies are growing on me," Bad said to no one in particular. "This is the most fun I've had in ages."

Darlington made a half-groan, half-growl. "I'm just going to shoot you and hope I have time to reload for Exile."

Minnie tsked. "No one is shooting anyone." Then she clapped her hands together, rather loudly, and Darlington grabbed both sides of his head.

Vice snorted a laugh while Bad grinned. Vice stepped up, peering at Darlington. "There's no way he could shoot anyone in this state. Couldn't hit the broad side of a barn."

Callum was still holding her close. She thought perhaps she should pull away, might make this conversation easier, but Callum's grip was rather firm and he was honestly quite nice to be pressed up against. She closed her eyes, drawing in his masculine scent.

Darlington straightened, his face pale, but his

gaze more resolute. "Would you care to test that theory?"

Vice took a half step back. "I was only teasing. There's no need for that."

Darlington turned toward Callum, pointing his finger. "You made us all promise at the start of this that we'd behave or you yourself would see that we married the girl we'd compromised."

Exile swallowed; she actually felt the vibration. "I did."

"What are your intentions toward Diana?" Daring had not dropped his hand.

Diana's breath caught. He was holding her in his arms, in front of everyone. She was trying not to, but she'd begun to hope that he'd offer for her hand. But instead of pulling her closer, he took a half step back, his hands dropping to his side. "I intend to keep her safe."

The air around her was cold without his heat and she clutched the blankets closer even as she lifted her head high. "Is that all?"

His eyes squinted. "Aye, lass."

She notched her chin higher. "I'm not your lass. Get out of my room."

CHAPTER SEVEN

Exile ground his teeth together as he stared at her, as she held the blankets about her with her straight shoulders and her head high. But her eyes, they told a different story and that tale made him wince.

They crinkled with hurt even as her mouth pinched into a frown.

"Ye can't just kick me out." He held out his hands on either side of him. "I'm to keep ye safe in case—"

"Get out!" she yelled so loudly that Daring clutched his head and Vice nearly fell over.

Minnie stepped up to her cousin, blocking Exile's view, and softy whispered something. Diana responded just as quietly.

Then Minnie turned to Exile. "It's time for you to leave."

"But…"

Minnie held up her hand. "Come with me." Then she started for the door. "You're to go back to bed." She patted Daring on the shoulder.

"I'm never drinking again," he mumbled, holding his head. "I think I shall die if I do."

Bad bent down to look Daring in the face. "The key is to drink more. Eventually, you'll outrun the hangover."

Minnie stopped, assessing Vice and Bad. Then she pulled the cord next to the door. "You both need some breakfast." Exile grimaced. So just he was in trouble. Not surprising the way he'd been holding Diana. Or perhaps the problem was what he'd done after.

Vice grinned. "That's the best idea I've heard so far. I like this woman."

Minnie raised a brow. "Then you will go home and sleep. Tomorrow at five sharp all three of you," her gaze cut to Exile, "are to return here. We've some things to discuss."

Exile could have smiled if the situation weren't so serious. Bad and Vice were in trouble too.

Daring straightened. "Excellent idea, love."

"I don't think so," Bad grumbled, standing up and crossing his arms. "No woman tells me—"

Daring growled, "Finish that sentence and I'll cut you from the club. I still own the controlling shares."

Bad pressed his lips together. "I don't need breakfast. Thank you very much."

"Fine," Minnie answered. "Suit yourself." She stepped up to Bad, staring into his face. "Plan on returning for dinner tomorrow." Then she pointed at Exile. "You're to follow me."

He did as he was told, giving Diana one last long look. She didn't meet his gaze, instead staring at the far wall. Her chin was still high, but it trembled a bit and regret lanced through his chest.

Did he tell her the truth? Somehow that seemed even worse. *I want you, but I'm promised to another.* What consolation was that really?

Minnie walked in front of him, not waiting or turning toward him until they'd gone down the stairs and entered a sitting room. "How drunk are you?"

"I beg yer pardon?" he asked, squinting at her as she pivoted in front of the fire to face him.

"You heard me. I don't want to have this conversation again. How drunk are you?"

He scratched the back of his neck. "I'm tired more than anything else."

She nodded. "I don't know how you feel about Diana."

His chest tightened. "I like her a great deal," he said. It was the truth.

Minnie let out a long breath, grasping the mantle. "But she's far more fragile than she likes to admit and, lately, she hasn't been herself."

Charles…that was the reason and if he'd had the chance, he'd see the man suffered for what he'd done. "I see."

"You're hurting her," Minnie said just loud enough to be heard. "Whether you mean to or not."

His throat went dry. "I have no intention—"

Minnie stepped toward him. "I don't give a heaping pile of dung about your intentions. You are causing her pain and that's what I care about. I know you're attracted to her, everyone knows it's true." She clasped her hands in front of her. "After Cordelia's incident, I agree that a guard needs to be kept, but you should not be keeping watch over my cousin unless you're considering marriage."

He winced. "Diana would make an excellent wife but…"

"But what?" she stepped closer.

He scrubbed his face. "My family has already arranged a match for me. I've never even met the lass."

"Does Diana know this?"

"No." he shook his head. "The end result is the same."

"Never even met her?" Minnie rubbed her chin. "You must not have any feeling for her whatsoever."

"What does that matter? It's my duty." He narrowed his gaze, trying to decide what she was thinking. He'd known the family long enough to know when a Chase woman was scheming. But her next words made him forget all about his suspicions.

"If we don't find Abernath soon then you'll have to pick one of the other men to trade with. If you truly can't take her for a wife, and you can't remain detached, it's best for both of you."

He straightened. One of the other men touching Diana? Escorting her about parties? His chest rumbled with jealousy and irritation. "Daring tried to trade. They won't." Her eyes widened at his words and he inwardly cursed. "He was worried about the feelings he was developing for you."

"I'm sure they'll switch. I'll see to it." Minnie looked back at the fire as though dismissing him.

He cocked his head, assessing her. "You and Diana are a great deal alike."

"We are," she answered with a pang of pride in her voice.

He rubbed his neck. "I ken ye're determined but I dinnae see either of them switching. For some reason, each man seems attached to his assignment." *Like the Chase women put a spell on us*, he thought to himself. He opened his mouth to share the joke with Minnie, but the glint of annoyance in her stare kept him from speaking.

Minnie's gaze swung back to him. "If either Vice or Bad touches a hair on Ada or Grace's neck I'll cut off their—"

"That's enough," Diana called from the doorway. He pivoted around, both relieved and suddenly nervous about her company. "I'd ask what you're discussing but I already know."

Exile held up his hands. "I was telling Minnie that we've been searching for Abernath, but it's difficult to find one woman in the sea of people who inhabit London. She's no' travelling in any of her normal circles."

Diana gave a stiff nod. "Thank you for your efforts." Then she turned to Minnie. "You can cease your interrogation. Lord Exmouth should return home and get some sleep."

Diana's hair was now braided and a dressing gown covered her lithe body. He wished he could hold the braid in his palm and allow his hand to trail over the silky hair. "O' course. Thank ye." He looked back at Minnie before he headed toward the door. Passing Diana, he pressed his hand to his side to keep from reaching for her. "I'll see ye soon."

She didn't answer nor did she look at him. "Goodbye, Lord Exmouth."

Inwardly, he cringed. He hated those words.

———

Diana stood next to Minnie, glaring at the side of her cousin's head as they stood in the foyer waiting for Lord Exmouth, Lord Baderness, and Lord Viceroy.

"If you continue to look at my wife with that expression, she may very well catch the plague." Daring rumbled from Minnie's other side.

Minnie grinned. "I shan't. I've weathered Diana's ire before."

Diana made a loud and audible harrumph. "Not like this, you haven't. Why am I having dinner with the man I already said goodbye to?"

Minnie sighed. "You've already asked and I've already answered. He has to trade with Vice or Bad."

"I don't need to be here for them to decide." Diana crossed her arms. "And now that I think about it. Neither does he. Also, I resent you hinting to mother that this was an attempt to match me with a suitor."

Minnie raised a single brow. "You do have to be here. Both Bad and Vice picked a Chase woman with a far gentler…nature. We must decide which one of them is capable of keeping you safe."

"In check, you mean." Diana stepped in front of Minnie. "And that still doesn't explain why Lord Exmouth needs to be here."

Diana saw it then. A tiny flinch in Minnie's gaze.

"Ha!" she yelled pointing at her cousin. "You are up to something."

Minnie put her hands on her hips. "I am not."

"You are too." Diana stepped closer tapping her chin. She stared at her cousin who began to blush. "You want to make him jealous. You think he'll offer for me if he is."

Minnie went from blush to pale. "How did you know that?"

"It worked with Daring. You think it will work again."

"Gads, Minnie," Daring said from Minnie's other side. "I thought you were the smartest woman I'd ever met but that was just frightening."

Diana looked over at her cousin's husband. Daring still looked pale from his night of debauchery. "How's your head? Still hurting?"

He gave her a wary eye, narrowing his gaze. "If I tell you are you going to use that information against me?"

Diana had to smile at that. "No. But I do want

you to discuss with your wife that she need not play matchmaker. I don't need her help."

"Everyone needs help sometimes, Diana. Even you." Minnie touched Diana's arm. "Please let me help you. A little."

Diana released a long breath she wasn't even aware she'd held. "Minnie. You don't understand everything that's happened."

Minnie scrunched her brow. "Then tell me. What's happened?"

Carriage wheels and the clopping of hooves sounded outside the estate. Diana spun around to face the door, giving her back to Minnie, her shoulders hunching in relief that she didn't have to answer her question. Minnie would surely think her terrible if she knew what she'd done with Charles.

Minnie's hand touched her shoulder, a gentle brush of her fingers. "You can tell me anything. You know that, right?"

Not this, Minnie looked down at the floor. "I know you mean well," she murmured.

"Diana," Minnie's voice pleaded a bit. "I know you haven't been yourself since we came back to London. What happened? Was it with Mr. Crusher?"

Diana tensed, hunching away from Minnie's touch. "Nothing happened."

Minnie paused and then wrapped a hand about

Diana's shoulder. "Since we were small girls balancing on your papa's knee or mine, we've been best friends. You know that you can trust me with anything. I love you as much as I love Ada or my mother and you know that I am strong enough to carry whatever burden you're facing. You don't have to do it alone."

Minnie's words pulled the air from her chest. But she didn't respond as the butler swung open the door and four men stepped inside.

Callum was at the front of the group. Her eyes were still on the floor, but she felt his entrance, like an invisible pull. She shifted her gaze to meet his and their eyes locked together. She held her breath, trying to remember how angry she was with him. Staring into his brown eyes made it so easy to forget.

"My lord," she said, curtseying quickly, heat filling her cheeks. She was glad to see him, she realized, and she honestly wished she didn't feel this way. It was easier to be angry at him considering he'd never propose to her despite his interest in her.

"My lady," he replied, giving a tight bow.

"And what other guests have you brought this evening?" Minnie asked from behind her, her voice coming up in short clipped tones.

Vice stepped forward. "This is my cousin, the earl

of Sinclair. He was hoping for an introduction with Your Grace." Vice winked.

Minnie stepped up next to her, tall and straight, her red hair shimmering in the evening light. "Her Grace does not remember inviting another guest."

Vice swallowed. "My apologies. I should have written."

"He's here now," Darlington answered, still behind her. "Welcome to our home, Lord Sinclair."

"Thank you, Your Grace," he replied, then stepped to the front of the group.

Diana blinked as she studied him. Vice was the most classically handsome man she'd ever met but his cousin somehow managed to be even more beautiful.

Rather than blond, he had dark hair and shimmering brown eyes set over a straight nose, full mouth, and a square jaw. He had broad shoulders and a tapered waist that might make a woman breathless.

Diana preferred the thick muscles of a burly Scot. One with reddish brown hair and the strong features that somehow filled her with warmth as well as desire, but still, Lord Sinclair was like a well-painted portrait, simply beautiful to look at but she had no desire to touch.

He looked at Minnie, giving a short bow. "Apologies, Your Grace, and thank you for your hospitality." Then he turned to Diana. His gaze lingered on her features for what seemed an excessively long time before he said, "My lady."

She nodded her head in response as she realized that Callum was inching closer, his shoulder now blocking Sinclair's view.

"Shall we make our way to the music room?" Minnie asked. "We've much to discuss and dinner will be upon us before we know it."

Diana followed her cousin, her heart hammering in her chest. She wasn't exactly sure what this evening was going to bring, but she had a feeling that whatever happened would change everything.

CHAPTER EIGHT

Exile stared at Diana's back as she walked next to the Earl of Sinclair. Even from behind, they made the perfect couple. His fists clenched. That should make him happy. He had a marriage contract. One that he needed to honor.

He closed his eyes. He didn't want to go through with marriage to Fiona. He'd received a letter from her the other day, he'd yet to open it. Which made his chest ache with guilt. Like he needed another reminder that he wasn't the man his cousin had been. Ewan would have never considered leaving the woman to whom he'd made a commitment. Honor and duty had always been his first concerns.

But damn, seeing Diana next to Sin made everything in him ache to punch that man directly in the face and carry Diana off the way his Scot ancestors might have.

He should be happy for her. She deserved a handsome, well-titled lord who could offer her the best sort of life. She was strong, kind, caring, and beautiful. She wasn't the sort of woman who should be shoved away by society. Instead, Diana should be leading other women on how to be intelligent and independent, not shoved on a shelf as she assumed.

He wished he could be the man to show her that. But then he spasmed with guilt again. He had his own demons that plagued him and a past that he needed to prove he was better than.

Perhaps he should give up on himself and focus on her. He was likely damned to hell anyhow.

Then he rubbed the back of his neck. She deserved better than a man who'd become earl because he'd allowed his cousin to die for him.

"What's the matter with you?" Daring murmured next to him.

Exile nearly jumped out of skin. He'd forgotten his friend was there. "Nothing."

Daring, looked over at him frowning, his face set in deep lines. "You're acting like a man who just committed a crime, or is being forced down the aisle at gunpoint."

Exile shook his head. "Are you going to force a

match between Diana and myself?" Part of him would be relieved. The decision would be out of his hands. But then he grumbled in dissatisfaction. That wasn't fair to either woman. Fiona shouldn't be ruined for his sake and Diana deserved a man who had chosen her.

What did he deserve? Probably a thrashing.

"No. Not yet." Daring touched his shoulder. "Should I?"

Exile gave a half smile. "No. Not yet."

"I know you're attracted to her," Daring said low and close to his ear.

"And?" He knew he was being intentionally obtuse, though the end result was the same. He couldn't marry Diana. He clenched his jaw. What would his friend think of his engagement? It was on the tip of his tongue to tell him and gain insight into possible solutions. But then he'd have to admit why he was engaged to Fiona and the circumstances around his cousin's death.

"And? Men have married for a lot less." Daring grabbed his shoulder, pulling him further behind the group. "We could be family, you big oaf."

Exile nearly laughed but it wasn't out of humor. "I can't marry Diana. Even if I wanted to, I…" He stopped. He couldn't hold the words back. "I've agreed to marry the woman promised to my cousin."

"Ewan?" Daring's mouth dropped open. "Christ." He patted Exile's shoulder. "I'm not familiar with Scottish customs. Would she be ruined if you didn't offer for her?"

Exile shook his head, holding in a sigh. Did he tell him that the blade that had killed Ewan had been meant for him? "No. But she was supposed to be a countess. I didn't want to take away her future. They'd been promised since they were children."

Daring's brow drew together. "And you felt this was your responsibility?"

Callum scrubbed one side of his face. "For a great many reasons, it is." She wrote to him regularly. Nothing very long or terribly personal. But she tried. More than could be said for him.

"And your feelings for Diana?" Daring tilted his chin down, giving Exile a long stare.

Exile shook his head. Daring didn't understand and wouldn't unless Exile told him the entire truth, which he likely never would. "Irrelevant."

The others rounded a corner but Daring didn't try to keep up. "Explain."

Exile shook his head. "We've fallen behind."

"It's my house." Daring gave him a dead stare. "I know where the bloody music room is. Explain."

He looked down at the floor. "I am responsible for my cousin's death."

"Hellfire and damnation," Daring swore under his breath. "You're not serious."

"I am." Exile swallowed. "I should have kept him safe, not endangered him."

Daring put both of his hands on Exile's shoulders. "Listen to me." Then he smacked his collarbone several times. "You didn't cut him with blade."

He shook his head. "Tell that to my aunt. She'll never forgive me."

Daring drew in a deep breath. "That is difficult." He dropped his hands. "I want you to think on this, though, because it is a thought I pondered often when considering Minnie. How much do you allow your past to affect your future?"

Exile shook his head. "Daring. I know ye mean well but I cannae undo my cousin's death nor could I be happy if I left Fiona adrift in the world."

Daring quirked a brow. "Is Fiona pretty?"

Exile snapped his mouth closed. "I don't ken I've never met her."

Daring's head reared back as he smacked his chest with his open palm. "You've never even met her? How were the arrangements made?"

Exile's face pulled taut. "My aunt made them by proxy. I dinnae like it, but I have to go through with the match. I want to be the sort of man on whom others can depend. Like Ewan was."

"I see." Daring's hand fell back to his side. "But marrying a woman you've never even met? What if we could find Fiona a suitable match? Then both women could credit you with providing for their future."

Exile cocked his head to the side. "Interesting idea. I hadn't thought of it." Then he shook his head. "I wish I were smarter like that. The club is the only way my lands even survive and even that wasnnae my design. It was yers."

Daring slapped him on the back as they began walking again. "Well, on that account, worry not. If you married Diana, she'd be full of ideas on how to make your estate more profitable. That woman is so smart, it frightens me—and I'm married to Minnie."

Exile drew in a deep breath as he puffed out his chest. Married to Diana? For one moment he allowed himself to dream of that possibility and it was glorious. But could he make that vision a reality?

DIANA SAT in the music room, shifting her chair as Lord Sinclair gave her another long look. His eyes twinkled with interest as he leaned closer, his shoulder subtly brushing hers. Nearby, Bad and Vice sat talking while Minnie sat herself down at the pianoforte and began to play.

Dear Lord, she should be enjoying the atmosphere but Sinclair's attention just made her uncomfortable. He was too handsome, too sparkly, too perfect. He almost seemed…fake.

And her body was intensely aware of another man, or at this moment, aware that he wasn't in the room. That he'd left her alone to flirt with a handsome, eligible earl.

A small sigh escaped Diana's lips. There was likely nothing wrong with Sinclair. The problem was her. She was flawed and she knew it, even if he didn't. She'd wondered why she'd allowed emotion to rule her heart when it came to Callum, but, of course, the answer was obvious. He didn't actually want her. That wasn't right, he wanted her physically, but he didn't actually wish to have a real relationship with her.

"Is everything all right, Lady Diana?" Sinclair asked, lightly touching the back of her hand.

She resisted the urge to snatch her hand away. "Fine, my lord. Thank you." She cleared her throat, trying to clear her feelings as well. "You've already asked after my family. Tell me about yours."

A shadow crossed the man's face. "I lost my wife, but I have a daughter who is my entire world."

That she could understand and, in that moment, she softened a bit. "My sisters and my family are more important than anything."

He gave a short nod, his shoulders straightening away from her as his hands rested on his thighs. "My daughter, Anne, is all the family I currently have and there isn't anything I wouldn't do for her."

Diana smiled, relaxing a bit. "I feel the same."

His eyes snapped to hers, all the twinkle gone. "How much would you risk to keep them safe?"

She cocked her head to the side. His demeanor had changed entirely. He'd gone from light and airy to stoic in a moment. "Odd question. Is she in trouble?"

His breezy smile returned. "Not at all. I guess, only having one family member, I sometimes wonder."

Diana studied him even as she attempted to return his smile. "There isn't anything I wouldn't sacrifice to keep them safe."

He leaned back in toward her. "That's what I like about you already. We're of the same mind."

She didn't respond. She supposed they were, and yet she didn't feel any connection to him whatsoever. Diana was spared answering as Callum and Daring entered the room. Her attention snapped to the large and brawny Scot as he filled the doorway.

His gaze narrowed as he stared back, looking from Sinclair back to her.

Minnie stopped playing. "You finally found your way," she called as she stood. "So glad we're all here."

Daring crossed the room, kissing her cheek as if it had been hours not minutes. "Sorry, my dear. What shall we do now that we're all here?'

"Oh, I think Diana should play for us." Minnie clapped her hands. "She's wonderful."

Diana turned to her cousin. "I'm passable." She stood, giving Minnie a glare. Her cousin was clearly meddling. "Really, you should play for us."

Minnie winked. A sure sign she was up to trouble. "Nonsense. Lord Viscount, would you be a dear and turn pages for her?"

"Me?" Vice scoffed. "Is there any scotch involved?"

Minnie let out a huff. "No, there is not."

"I'd be happy to turn pages for you." Sinclair stood, holding out his elbow. "Shall we?"

"Don't be ridiculous," Callum called from across the room. "I'll turn the pages."

Diana knew one thing for certain. Minnie's meddling was going to lead to trouble.

CHAPTER NINE

Exile stomped across the room, making himself as tall as possible. He wanted Sin to know that he was a large man and people generally didn't tangle with him.

Sin's brows pushed together as he gave Exile a long look. Exile knew what question the man would ask if Diana wasn't standing there. He'd say, why are you doing this?

Exile had been clear in the carriage on the ride over that one of the other men needed to trade Chase ladies with him. But that conversation had been for Bad and Vice. They were his longtime friends, they knew the seriousness of the situation, they—and he couldn't stress this enough—had no interest in Diana beyond their duty to the club and their friends.

But Lord Sinclair was another matter entirely. The man seemed keenly interested in getting attached to an earl's daughter. Diana was beautiful, and well-heeled, but still something didn't feel right. Perhaps it was how quickly he'd stationed himself at Diana's side.

Even when a man was attracted to a woman, he was more likely to observe for a bit, see if her personality suited him. Or perhaps Exile was wrong and only he did that sort of thing?

He ticked back through all his friends. They resisted love and marriage like the plague. And here was Sinclair, practically throwing himself at Diana. He must have some ulterior motive.

Was he in need of funds and looking to tap into Diana's dowry? Exile's lips thinned. She wasn't some prize, she was an amazing woman.

He reached Diana's side and held out his elbow. Somewhere in his walk across the room, he'd decided it was his duty to protect her from whatever intentions Sin had. Or perhaps he was simply indulging his own jealousy. "Lady Diana."

She gave him a puzzled look as she placed her hand in his elbow. "Lord Exmouth."

He ignored the little voice that reminded him he'd come here for the exact opposite reason. Rather than taking on additional protection, he was supposed to be handing her guard off to another man.

They moved to the pianoforte and he helped her onto the bench, stationing himself over her shoulder, leaning close and allowing his breath to blow across the back of her neck.

"What are you doing?" she half hissed, half whispered.

He cocked one of his brows. "What do ye mean?"

"You know what I mean." Her gaze narrowed. "Tell me what's the matter with you."

He dropped the eyebrow. She was getting to know him too well to lie. "I dinnae like him."

"Who?" she asked, suddenly looking away and shuffling through the pages of the book to select a song.

Liar, he thought as he leaned closer, his arm brushing hers. He was beginning to understand her too. "Ye ken who."

She slapped the book on the stand. "Try to keep up."

"I've been trying to do that since I met ye," he mumbled back, but she heard him anyway and turned to look at him.

"You have?" There was a question in her eyes and he wanted to answer by kissing her right here in front of everyone, claiming her for his own. He looked over at Daring who was staring longingly at his wife, his gaze unwavering from Minnie. That was how Exile felt about Diana.

She started the notes of the song, and he started in surprise. The piece was a high, clear Highland song that echoed through the room with haunting beauty.

He couldn't move as the music traveled through him, touching his soul. It was exactly like Diana, so perfect for him. She embodied the same deep, soulful beauty that left him breathless with desire and…. He leaned over to turn the page and his arm brushed hers, making her fingers slip on keys. Rather than ruin the music for him, the sound only amplified his feelings. He had a definite effect on her. He drew in her fresh scent as one of her loose hairs tickled his cheek.

He wished he could pull her into his lap, hold her close, and tell her that he loved her. He was in love with her. The revelation stole his breath as he reached over to turn the page again. Hellfire and damnation, no wonder he couldn't stand to see Sinclair flirt with her.

Then his heart constricted. It didn't change the promise he'd made to Fiona or the one he'd made to his aunt to honor Ewan's life. He'd do well to find

Fiona a new match before declaring his affection for Diana. It only seemed right.

He squeezed his eyes shut. What if she moved on before he accomplished his plan for Fiona? How was he going to watch Diana with another man? Yes, he knew her secret and he knew that Diana believed she wouldn't marry—but she would. She was full of too much life to be passed by.

Perhaps he needed to return to his home and claim his bride.

He looked over at Bad and Vice. Even they'd known he was not going to stay at the club long, that's why they'd brought in Sinclair in the first place. But it felt as though Sin was taking over his life. His friends, his club, his place next to Diana.

His shoulders straightened. His aunt had often told him that his allegiance to his life in England was a problem. The last visit he'd made two years prior, she'd said to him, "Come home. Live here like ye were meant to."

He'd disagreed. The money he made in London kept the farms well-stocked and the tenants fed. She'd frowned. "Ewan would have done the same but he'd have provided for them in Scotland, where he could also give them his attention."

Callum sighed. She was right, she'd always been right. He wasn't the man Ewan had been and his love for Diana only underscored that fact. She wasn't the perfect Scottish bride he should want. But he did want Lady Diana Chase with all his heart and soul.

The notes of Diana's song died slowly, echoing through the music room and his chest. "That was beautiful, lass."

She turned to him, her mouth soft but pulled down at the corners. "The song made me think of you."

He brushed her shoulder as he thought of Daring's words. Was there a way to care for Fiona and still keep Diana for himself? He knew that he was being selfish, but he wanted her for himself. His fingertips tingled with the hope that thought brought. "Have ye ever been to the Highlands?"

She shook her head. "I'd like to. You told me once that I'd make a good Scottish bride. I think I'd like it there."

"I think ye would too," he whispered.

But his heart said more. It softly murmured that he was going to take her there and make love to her in a field of heather. "Do ye ride?"

Her breath caught. "It's my favorite."

Of course it was. "We'll go. We'll ride for hours and take a picnic and ye—"

She drew her brows together, his face spasming with pain. "Now you're being cruel."

Was he? He likely was. What he was less certain of was who he was hurting most. Because his aunt had been right about him all along. He was selfish and not half the man Ewan had been. He stood then just as Sin crossed the room.

"That was lovely," he gushed smiling. "Play another. I'll turn the pages for you this time."

Callum puffed out his chest. Whatever the consequences, his mind had been made up. Diana would stay at his side no matter the consequence. He'd find another husband for Fiona. Sin was not getting on this bench.

Diana knew male posturing when she observed it. She'd once had a pair of hounds that had behaved the same way. They had circled and growled, sniffed and nipped, a bone between them.

Diana was no man's bone.

She stood, stepping in front of Callum. "Thank you, Lord Sinclair. I may play again in a bit. Right now, I'd love to spend time with all of you. It's not often I have such interesting dinner company."

Callum rumbled behind her, the sound echoing deep in his throat.

She tried not to grin but one corner of her lip

pulled up. He'd hurt her yesterday with his rejection and while she didn't want him to really suffer, it satisfied her to know he hurt a little too.

"Wonderful idea," Sinclair said as he held out his elbow.

She reached out her fingers just as a hand came to her back. "I agree," Callum said, his large fingers spread across the small of her back, filling her with heat. "There's a settee near the window that is perfect for two."

Callum swung her around, leaving Sinclair to trail behind. "Or three," the other man added, not giving up.

Dogs...bone, she thought with a sigh. "Really, shouldn't we join His Grace?"

"No," both men said at once. She started in surprise looking back at Sinclair then at Callum. Callum cracked his knuckles while Sin clenched his teeth.

Diana, for her part, attempted to catch Minnie's eye but she, Daring, Bad, and Vice had their heads bent together in deep discussion.

She craned her neck, trying to attract Minnie's attention but it was for naught. Minnie never looked up.

They reached the settee and Callum nearly spun her around, like a man might on the dance floor so that she sat with a hip against the arm of the couch, then he took the seat next to her, only leaving room for Sinclair on his other side. But the man walked around, leaning his leg against the arm of the couch and brushing Diana's shoulder.

"Tell me, Lady Diana, will you participate in the upcoming season? It will begin soon." Lord Sinclair asked, attempting to speak around Callum's large frame.

Callum leaned closer, his hip pressing into hers. She was starting to feel imprisoned. "Of course. My sister, Emily, has married the Earl of Effington and my sister, Cordelia, the Marquess of Malicorn. My parents will be anxious for me to come out."

Callum looked down at her. "You haven't had a season?"

She shook her head. "No. Emily hadn't wed until recently, so this will be my first."

"Your sisters both made excellent matches." Sin leaned out so that he might look at her, his chest nearly touching his knees.

Her head cocked to the side and Callum bent close to her ear and muttered, "He's already counting yer dowry."

She blinked, looking at her large, surly Scot.

"I beg your pardon?" Sinclair straightened. "What did you say?"

Callum didn't respond, instead he pressed closer to her. "There is more room next to Lord Baderness."

Sinclair narrowed his eyes. "Really? There seems to be plenty of room over here."

Diana drew in a deep breath, trying to remember how she'd kept her dogs from hurting each other all those years ago. "I do believe you're right. There is more room over there." Without another word, she stood and crossed the room, taking the seat next to Bad.

Bad looked over at her with one brow scrunched low. She shrugged. "Those two have decided they must puff their chests and…"

Bad gave her a smile. It wasn't the smile like he'd had when he was drunk. This one was nice, lighting his whole face. It softened him, made him actually approachable. "Acting like a couple of cocks in a henhouse, are they?"

She let out a little giggle, "In my head, I thought they were like two hounds I had once who would disagree over the stew bone."

Bad nodded. "That's a good one." Then he scratched his chin. "I see it, they're over there locking horns still like a couple of old goats."

She giggled all the more. "I didn't realize you were funny, my lord. Thank you for the bit of humor. It was lovely."

He jerked his chin down in a quick nod. "I could say the same for you. Can I ask you why your other cousin and sister aren't here?"

"Ada and Grace?" She straightened. "Minnie and I made them stay home. It's safer."

"But aren't you in danger?" He squinted his eyes, studying her.

She shrugged. "I'll be fine. They need to be protected. In different ways, they are softer, gentler women. Whatever will happen, it's happening to me, not them."

Bad stared at her. "I begin to understand why Exile likes you so much." Then he turned to Lord Darlington. "Daring. I shall look out for Lady Diana."

"Excellent." Darlington slapped his hands together. "That was easier than I thought it might be."

"The hell it was," Exile boomed. "I've changed my mind, I'm up to the task myself."

He is acting like a child, Diana thought as she turned to him. "You are not," she replied, straightening her spine.

He stood. "I am."

"Fear not." Lord Sinclair straightened too. "I can help with this situation."

"The only help we want from ye is to watch ye

leave." Exile turned to Sinclair, his nose dropping within an inch of the other man's.

"Cocks," Bad said again.

"What's that?" Vice asked.

"You two." Daring pointed at Exile and Sinclair. "Follow me to my study."

"I'm fine here," Exile rumbled, crossing his hands over his chest.

"I'm not asking. Now," Daring said as he turned and began to march toward the door. "Or the back we'll be watching will be yours."

Exile stomped across the room, as he did, he looked at her. "I need to speak with ye tonight."

She raised her brow. "I'd worry about the angry duke first." But a niggle of hope wriggled about her stomach. Had Minnie been right after all? Did she have a chance for a love match with Exile?

CHAPTER TEN

Exile stormed down the hall. He'd been to Spain once when they'd run with the bulls. The matadors would wave a red flag in front of the bull, inciting its anger. That's how he felt now. Like the bull, he wanted to thrust his horn into any man who got between him and Diana.

Daring turned into an open door and Exile followed, Sin just behind him. Daring took a seat behind his desk. "Sit," he told both of them.

Exile considered refusing but then took a seat. Sin sat just to his right. The man lowered himself in the chair, and Exile noticed a stiffness in his movements. "Do ye box?" he asked.

Sin frowned. "Why? Are you hoping to challenge me in the ring?" He settled his back into the plush leather. "The answer is no."

"Do ye ride? Or did ye suffer from a fall?"

The man's face paled. "I don't know what you're talking about."

"Never mind." Daring waved his hand. "Sin, is that what they're calling you?"

Sinclair nodded. "It is."

"I give you more trust than most since you're family to Vice but with all due respect, we don't know you. There is no chance we will leave Diana's safety in your hands."

Exile relaxed back into his chair.

"As for the club, please return here tomorrow for us to discuss the possibility of you purchasing a share." Darlington leaned back, crossing one ankle over his knee.

Exile rubbed the back of his neck. "Why did I have to be here for ye to say that?"

Daring gave him a long look then turned back toward Sinclair. "Diana would be most protected if she were married. If you are interested, I will see that she is returned to her home tomorrow in time for her normal calling hours."

Exile shot forward in his chair. "You dirty piece of—"

"Lord Exile has been clear that he doesn't wish to propose." Daring gave his friend an angelic grin.

"That isnae what I said and ye had offered up a

suggestion to untangle my situation." He gripped the arms of his chair.

Daring shook his head. "We don't have forever for you to decide. Unless, of course, we can find Lady Abernath. I've gotten some reports of her being sighted near St. James Square. With any luck, I'll find her and then you're free to take as long as you wish."

Exile slapped his hands on the leather. "Ye're no' free to just meddle like this in someone else's affairs."

"I am." Daring tented his fingers in front of his chin. "In fact, Diana is my family now. I've far more right than you."

The frustrating part was that Daring was correct.

Sinclair drummed his fingers on the armchair. "You've seen her by Saint James Square?" Sin asked. "How long ago?" The man's attention had become keen. Exile wrinkled his brow, wondering why.

"Yesterday." Daring sat straighter. "Why?"

That was what Exile wanted to know as well.

Sin's eyes widened. "No reason." He gave a tight smile. "So I am free to court Lady Diana if I wish?"

"Yes," Daring answered.

At the same moment, Exile growled, "No." Thinking of Diana made him forget all about Abernath.

Sin pointed a finger at Exile. "His Grace just told you that the decision is his, not yours."

Exile knocked the finger away from his face. Sin winced, pulling the hand toward his body.

"What's the matter with ye?" Exile asked, looking the man over. A light slap of the hand should not have warranted that sort of response.

"Nothing," Sin snapped back. Then he stood. "Your Grace, I know that I arrived unannounced. I look forward to our meeting tomorrow, but I will take my leave so you can get on with the rest of your evening." Then the man turned and left.

Daring glared across the desk. "Are you happy?"

"No," he answered. Something, but he couldn't quite put his finger on it, was terribly wrong. His chest tightened. Yes, he was jealous and honestly worried about Sin's interest in Diana. But more than that, his gut churned. Danger was in the air.

―――

Diana sat in the music room, chatting with Vice and Bad. She had to confess, she liked them both. Most unexpected.

They'd been funny, polite, and easy company. Not only that, but they had some rather colorful stories.

"So there we were, sleeping in a barn, in the

middle of Essex, in the dead of winter." Vice slapped his knee. "Can you believe that?"

She shook her head. "Part of me wants to applaud you for surviving." She covered her mouth with her hand. "How did you not freeze to death?"

Vice shrugged. "The brandy of course. Drank half the shipment I was supposed to be delivering."

She pressed her hand more firmly against her lips to keep from howling with laughter. "Oh, you are a funny one."

"Lady Diana." Lord Sin came crashing back through the door. "May I have a word with you?"

"A word?" she asked, looking at Vice. In reply, Vice shrugged and turned to his cousin.

"Is everything all right?" Vice asked.

Sin stopped, his features becoming less heavy. "Of course. His Grace has agreed to have me look after Diana. I'd just like her to go over possible outings she has in the next week so that I might clear my schedule. Perhaps we could step out onto the terrace?" He gave her a winning smile. "We need not bore the others."

She nibbled her lip as she assessed him. Somehow, that didn't seem right. He wasn't part of their arrangement, he was new to the group. And Exile… he really just gave up that easily?

Her shoulders drooped. "Of course."

Vice stood too. "I'll come as well."

"No need." Sin held up his hand. "Stay here and enjoy. We'll be just outside the doors where you can see us. It's a fine spring night." Then he grabbed her hand and tucked it in his elbow.

Diana looked back at Minnie, who looked equally confused, her fingers pressed to her cheek. "You'll stay where we can see you."

"Yes, Your Grace," Sin called back as they stepped through an open door.

The fresh air tickled her skin and the evening was lovely. "Daring actually agreed to have you keep watch?"

"Yes," he answered, not stopping but continuing to cross the open patio. "There was some conversation between him and Exile earlier where Exile confessed why he couldn't do so himself."

Wait. What did that mean? She'd thought this was her idea.

"And as I am becoming a partner at the club…"

"Oh, I see," she answered, but the night got darker as they moved from the candlelight. "We should stop, they won't be able to see us."

He continued on, pulling her faster still. "That's all right. There is something I want to show you."

This situation got stranger by the second. Apprehension trickled down her spine. "Show me?" she asked. The garden gate sat just to her right and she heard the whinny of horses. "Horses in the alley this time of night?" Diana pulled to a stop. "I-I should go back."

"Not yet." He gave her a winning smile. "I have a confession to make. We've already met."

She shifted uncomfortably. Her feet tingled with the urge to leave. "I don't recognize you."

"Well, you wouldn't."

She swallowed as she tried to pull her hand from his arm but his other hand clamped down over hers. "What do you mean? What's happening?"

He grimaced. "The first time we met, I was wearing a mask."

"What?" She drew in a breath to let out a scream. That's when a bag dropped over her head.

CHAPTER ELEVEN

Exile sat across from Daring, but his eyes were unfocused as he rubbed his jaw. Some idea flitted around the edge of his thoughts but he couldn't quite hold onto it. Sin's entrance into their life had been so sudden and his interest in Diana so immediately intense.

"What's the matter with you?" Daring leaned forward, waving his hand in front of Exile's face.

Exile blinked, focusing on his friend. "Something isnae right with Vice's cousin."

"He's fine. You're jealous," Daring grunted, sitting back.

Exile pushed off the desk, rising from his chair. "I dinnae think so." He shook his head. "His interest is unnatural this soon."

"She's the most classically beautiful woman I've

TAMMY ANDRESEN

ever seen and that's saying something. I've seen a lot of women.'"

"True." Exile stared out the window into the night. "But he suddenly appeared and he's part of our actual business and now our dealings with Abernath and I barely touched his arm and he flinched." Like he had a wound…perhaps running down his side. "Bloody fecking Christ!" he yelled, barreling for the door.

"What?" Daring asked, jumping from his desk and chasing after him.

His gut churned even as his hands clenched into fists. "He's wounded on his left side. The attack in the alley. I slashed the man with my right hand…his left."

"No," Daring said low and deep. "It can't be. He's Vice's cousin."

"We're about to find out." Exile skidded to a stop in front of the music room and threw open the door. The scene before him made his pause.

Minnie, Bad, and Vice sat laughing and talking. But Sin and Diana were nowhere to be seen. He marched forward, his gaze swinging between one wall to the other, and his heart skipped a beat when he found no one else in the room. Sweat slicked his forehead, and his gut clenched. Where the hell was Diana?

"Where are they?" He barked, his eyes pinging all over the room.

"What?" Minnie squinted at him. "Oh, they're just out on the terrace. Sinclair wanted her schedule for the next week so that…" But she stopped as she looked outside into the empty dark.

"Minnie," Daring's voice held an edge. "What are you talking about? Why would he need her schedule?"

Exile's chest tightened as his breath came in short gasps. Crossing the room, he headed for the doors.

"He's going to take Exile's place. Make sure Lady Abernath doesn't attempt to hurt her the way she did with Cordelia."

Daring slammed his fist on the table as Exile stepped outside, picking up speed. *Please let her be in the garden*, he prayed.

Daring's voice followed him out. "He isn't guarding her. I would never agree to that."

"Help me look," he yelled, starting down a path. Then another. It wasn't until he got to the gate that he noticed a piece of ribbon on the path which looked exactly like the ones that had adorned Diana's hair.

"Anything?" Vice called, coming up behind him.

He reached down and picked up the single scrap of fabric. "I found this by the gate." His voice was scratchy. How long had he been in the office? Mere minutes. "If he's taken her, they can't have gotten far."

"Taken her?" Vice waved them off. "Sinclair would never take Diana, he's here to help."

Exile spun around, grabbing his friend by the collar and slamming him to the wall. He didn't have time to be nice. "Did you approach him or did he come to ye?"

Vice's face paled. "He came to me. But that doesn't mean…"

"I dinnae have time to convince ye. He's taken the woman I love. And I need her back. Where would he go?"

Vice shook free as Bad came up behind them.

"He wouldn't," Vice answered holding his head.

"We can debate later," Bad replied, attempting to hold back his anger and panic. "They came out into the garden and now they are gone. Daring is having the house searched. But we are going out on horseback. Where are we going Vice? Think."

"He's got a small townhouse. I suppose we should start there."

"Good," Exile answered, drawing in what felt like the first breath in minutes. "I'll have the horses saddled, we leave momentarily."

It felt good to be doing something. Good to have

a plan. Because he had to find her. He'd only just realized what she meant to him.

Diana sat in a carriage, the hood still over her head, her hands tied behind her back. The man was going to pay for this. She'd done her best to kick and fight, but Sin and another man had trussed her up and shoved her into a small buggy. Now she heard the clop of the horses and could feel the carriage's wheels move as she struggled to sit up.

"Here, let me help you," Sin said close by. Strong hands lifted her up from her position of half laying across a seat to sitting.

"Don't touch me," she said, though her voice was muffled. He reached for the hood and pulled it off her face.

He was close and for a brief second, she thought about spitting in his face. She settled for sneering. "Why are you doing this?"

He cringed. "I'm sorry. I don't want to hurt you."

"But you're going to anyway." Diana tested the bindings on her wrists. Neither man was good at knots apparently because the ties were neither tight nor well-knotted. They immediately began to loosen.

He held up his hands. "This would have been easier if Exile hadn't thwarted my first attempt. Then I wouldn't have to know you when I took you."

Her bindings came undone but she kept her hands behind her back. Diana had already puzzled out that he was the man that had attacked them in the alley. Which meant he had a nice cut on his side. "I'm so sorry for you," she said, her voice dripping with sarcasm.

He grimaced. "That came out wrong. Please try to understand. She's taken my daughter."

Diana stopped, her stomach dropping. She remembered his comments earlier about family. He'd been trying to explain. "You're doing this to get her back."

"I am." He leaned forward and that's when she saw his walking stick sitting on the seat next to him. "You seem lovely, Diana, but Anne is my child. She's everything to me. And with her mother gone, it's my job to see her raised and to keep her safe."

Diana moved closer, configuring her face into one of sympathy. "I understand."

Surprise lit his face. "You do?"

She nodded, scooting further off the bench, keeping her hands hidden. "You'd do anything for her."

He nodded eagerly. "I thought about asking

Daring or Vice for help, but I can't risk it. What if Lady Abernath finds out and hurts—"

Diana grabbed the stick and not having time to bring it down on his head, she jabbed him hard in the left ribs where she knew he was wounded.

He made a groaning sound of pain as he slumped to the side. Quick as a snake, she took the handle and knocked him in the head. He bounced off the wooden frame with the other side of his skull, making a loud thud.

"Eh. What was that?" the driver called, pulling the horses to a stop.

Diana drew in a sharp breath as she pushed Sin to the floor. Then she braced her feet and held the cane the way a man might a rapier.

Her hands began to sweat on the wood as the seat squeaked and feet landed on the ground. "I asked, what was that?" The moment the door opened she made a sharp jab right in the man's stomach. His eyes bulged as he doubled over clutching his middle. Without pause, she brought the cane down on the back of his head. He dropped like a stone to the ground.

Diana didn't hesitate. She hopped out over him and then climbed in the driver's seat. "Hey-ya," she yelled as she picked up the reins and gave them a snap. The door was still open but she wasn't sure she cared if Sin tumbled out. Then again, they might want to question him.

Pulling the carriage to a stop, she hopped down as her evening dress made a decided tearing noise. She sighed. She rather liked this dress. But she'd get another. Snapping the door closed, she climbed back into her seat. Now to find her way back to Daring's estate.

CHAPTER TWELVE

Exile climbed into the saddle of his horse, anxious to get started. "Ye said he lives off of Bow Street?" Damn, he'd hoped the man was closer.

"Yes, but…" Vice stopped, pointing down the alley. "What's that?"

Exile squinted into the darkness. A carriage rolled toward them as the driver waved. "What the…"

He leaned forward. Was that Diana driving the carriage? His heart hammered in his chest. She was okay. More than that, she was Diana. Strong, brave, and driving a carriage through the streets of London. Exile loved that woman with his whole heart.

"Callum," she called, waving again. "Hurry before he wakes."

"Did she…" Bad started, his head cocking to the side.

"She did," Exile said, a large grin spreading across his face. Pride expanded in his chest. "She rescued herself."

Diana rolled closer just as the door to the carriage snapped open and Sin tumbled out onto the cobblestone.

The man pulled himself from the ground, stumbling as he held his side and made his way back down the alley. Baring his teeth, Exile kicked his horse and started after the man. He'd pay for what he's done.

Sin moved faster but Exile gained on him and he raised his crop ready to strike. The man had attempted to steal his life away, the same way that thug at the tavern had taken his cousin. He wished he'd made that man pay but now he had the chance to see this wrong righted.

"Stop," Diana shouted, holding up her hand.

He yanked the reins. "This bastard deserves a good beating."

"Trust me, I took care of him." She fired back. "Now draw your pistol and tie him up."

Exile looked at her through the haze of anger clouding his sight. He wanted to hurt the man.

Bad drew up next to him. "Let me by," he yelled,

even as he pulled out his derringer. "Stop, Sin, or I'll be forced to fire."

Exile shimmied his horse to the side as Bad raced passed him, easily subduing the man on foot.

Sin raised his hands. "Please. Please don't kill me. She's depending on me."

Vice made his way by as well, jumping from his steed to help Bad tie the other man's hands.

"Who?" Exile barked, getting down from his horse. "Abernath?"

"No." Diana hopped down from the seat of the carriage, looking as though she'd done the task every day of her life. "His daughter. Abernath is blackmailing Sin into helping her by stealing his child."

Exile stopped, some of the fog clearing. "What?"

Diana touched his arm. "Try to understand. What would you do if someone stole away the person you loved?"

He looked at her. How did he tell her that he loved her? And his heart had nearly broken when he'd discovered her gone? What was more, this wasn't the first time. "I'd do almost anything."

She touched his arm, smiling up at him. "I know. Me too."

"He tried to hurt ye," Exile answered, not happy with standing here watching Bad and Vice do the work.

Not that Vice looked happy either. His face was twisted in pain. "How could you betray my friends? I trusted you."

"Sin's secret is out." Diana lightly massaged his arm. "He can't make good on his attempt to take me. But we can gain access to Abernath through him, Callum. We'll need him awake to get information out of him."

He shook his head. "Ye are ridiculously smart. How did ye overcome him?"

She blushed a bit. "He thought my hands were tied. I used his walking stick." Then she started. "Oh. And I left the driver somewhere on Somerset Street crumpled in a ball."

Exile grabbed her then, pulling her against his chest. "Ye knocked out two men?"

She looked up at him, her eyebrows cocked. "Don't hurt my feelings, Callum. I'm not a woman to be trifled with."

He laughed then. "I can see that, love."

"Love?" she asked, her fingers spreading out on his chest.

"Yes. Love," he answered as he swooped down to take her lips in a kiss. "I was so frightened for ye."

She shook her head. "I've already told you. I can take care of myself."

He brushed away a stray curl from her face. His

heart aching as he looked down at her. "The strongest man I knew died in my arms after he'd been shot. He was better than me in every way except the one instance where I moved and he didn't." Exile's chest ached. "If only I had pushed him or yelled a warning, or…" He squeezed her tighter.

Diana slid her arms about his neck. "You didn't know."

He shook his head. "I'll tell ye the whole story and then ye can judge. But I knew. And I assumed he did too."

Bad and Vice came by him, leading Sin back into the gate.

"Please," Sin said again. "Do whatever you want to me, but please help my daughter."

"Damn it," Exile swore under his breath. Because Diana was right. The man was desperate and their only hope of finding Abernath. "Ye and I are going to have a little chat," he growled out.

Sin gave a nod as he looked to Diana. "Help me save her."

Diana squeezed Exile tighter about the neck. "Of course we will."

"We?" he asked, looking down at her.

"We," she answered, notching her chin.

Over his dead body. There was no way he'd allow

her to be at risk again. Now that he'd had her back, he wouldn't lose her.

DIANA WATCHED HIS JAW TIGHTEN. She lifted her own higher in response. She had a plan and it definitely required her own participation. Callum was going to have to deal with her too.

He let out a growl of dissatisfaction as he loosened one arm from around her waist so that he could propel her toward the garden gate. "Ye're not getting any more involved in this than ye've already been. It's too dangerous."

"I have every intention of protecting my sister and cousin. I'd like to see this all end and so I will do whatever I have to do."

He stopped. "Diana." Her name came out as a plea. "Try to understand. I lost the most important person in my life. I…" He drew in a breath, then exhaled it slowly. "I got into a fight with a man outside a tavern when he tried to steal my horse. I refused to back down and my cousin, Ewan, the rightful Earl of Exmouth, backed me up. I should have known a horse thief would fight until the bitter end, it's a hanging offense. But I wanted what was mine. When the bugger swiped at me with his blade, I ducked out of the way, but Ewan…he dinnae.."

Diana shook her head. She could hear the pain tightening his voice. "That's awful."

"I should never have started that fight. And I should have protected him. I—"

She held a finger to his lips. "You can't blame yourself."

He furrowed his brow. "Ye heard my story."

She nodded, then raised up to place a light kiss on his lips. "I did. You are not responsible for that man's actions."

He frowned. "Tell that to my aunt. She'll never forgive me for his death."

Diana shook her head. "That's her grief talking."

"What if something happened to Ada or Grace and ye could have prevented it?" he asked.

Diana's chest constricted. "You're right. I'd never forgive myself."

Somehow, that made him relax. "So you see why I blame myself for Ewan's death."

She gave a nod. She did understand.

"And why I can't let you get any more involved." He leaned his forehead against hers. "I love you, Diana. I cannae let anything happen to ye."

"You…you love me?" Her insides turned to warm puddles of wax. "Truly?"

"I do. Now say ye'll stay out of this."

Diana squinted up at him. It wasn't a declaration of a future but to know that he felt as she did was heartwarming. Still, she couldn't allow her feelings to keep her from doing the right thing. "I can't. For Ada and Grace's sake, I need to see this done. I thought you understood too."

He dropped his hands, wanting to wrap them around her. "I'll take care of all of ye. I promise."

"I'm not the woman who is going to sit on the side and allow you to rescue me. You know that." Her fingers balled into fists.

He brought his hands to his hips giving her a pointed stare. "Of course I do. But I'm no' the kind of man who'll allow a woman I love to run headlong into danger."

She slowly uncurled her fingers and reached up to touch his cheek. "If you want to love me, you have to love all of me." Then she turned and started for the house. "I have a plan. Are you at least willing to listen?"

"Do ye know what's most annoying about ye," he grumbled behind her, but his hand brushed her back.

"I can think of many traits that might qualify as most annoying." She tossed him a grin over her shoulder.

He gave a single laugh. "The worst is how often ye're right."

That made her stop and she looked back at him. "Huh. I wouldn't have picked that one. I thought that was one of my finer qualities."

"Are we going to get his daughter back too?" He drew her closer again, dropping his nose into her hair.

"Yes, and we're not even going to kill him. At least not yet."

That made him chuckle. "I'm so glad ye're safe. Ye are miraculous."

She squeezed his middle again. "You're pretty miraculous too."

Minnie came rushing out the doors. "Diana," she cried, racing toward them as she lifted her skirts. "Can you ever forgive me?"

Diana looked at him. "Minnie, there is nothing to forgive. You couldn't have known." Those words were for Exile as much as they were for Minnie.

His eyes crinkled in pain. "Thank ye, lass."

Minnie wrapped her in a hug. "How did you get away?"

"I'll tell you in just a few. For right now, we need to plan a rescue."

CHAPTER THIRTEEN

EXILE TRIED NOT to sigh but a half breath came out. "No' a rescue. A capture."

Diana waved her hand. "Yes, of course." He was fairly certain that she was placating him.

He didn't say a word this time, just followed. He'd listen to her and figure out what she was thinking, then he'd decide how to best protect her. Because, whatever anyone else's goals were, that was his. Keeping Diana safe.

Minnie twined her arm with Diana's. "How did you get away?"

"She clubbed Sin with his own walking stick," Exile said, his insides feeling a bit lighter. She was right. Diana was exceptionally good at taking care of herself. "Then she beat the driver. Speaking of, let's send Bad back to see if he cannae capture that man too."

"Good idea," Diana answered.

Bad and Vice hadn't made it far. Daring was in the music room, the three men tying Sin to a pianoforte bench.

Exile crossed the room and, ignoring Sin, turned to Bad. "See if ye can find the driver." Then he looked at the other man. "Who was he?"

"He worked for Lady Abernath." Sin swallowed. "He was supposed to help me, but I'm sure he was a watchman instead. Making sure I did what I was told."

"I'll go with him," Vice volunteered, giving his cousin a look of disgust.

"Hurry," Exile said.

They headed back out onto the veranda, breaking into a run.

Exile looked at Diana. "What do ye want to ask?"

"I beg your-—" Daring started, but Exile held up his hand. Now was not the time for his friend to pull the Duke rank.

Diana stepped up and rather than lean over Sin, she sat next to him. "Tell us everything."

"Like what?" Sin gave her a wary eye, his shoulders slumping.

"When did your daughter disappear?"

Sin looked at the floor. "Four days ago. But that isn't the beginning." He closed his eyes. "I owed Lady Abernath money."

Diana grimaced and Exile surely looked the same. Bad stories often started with such a statement. "She came to me because she needed the funds repaid. I didn't have them." He shook his head. "My reasons for wanting to join the club are my own, I needed that money for an investment."

Diana touched Sin's arm. Exile felt another niggle of jealousy. Why did she need to give this man sympathy? Then again, Sin also had a large egg forming on his head. "And when you couldn't repay her?"

"The driver is her most trusted servant. I can't prove it, but I believe he stole my daughter from our home even as Lady Abernath and I were talking."

"It wouldn't be the first time," Daring mumbled.

Sin squeezed his eyes shut. "I realized moments after Abernath had left. My nanny hurtled into my office, crying that she couldn't find Anne. We searched for hours until we got a note." He raised his eyes. "Abernath was clear. You for her. It was after midnight and the missive said you were at the club. When I failed, she told me to try and join the ranks to get close to you, Diana. Please. I know what I did was wrong but I just wanted Anne back. My daughter is all I have in this world. She's everything."

Diana nodded her thoughts turning over a plan. "And tonight? What were you to do with me?"

Sin scrubbed his face, pain and worry pinching his features. "I was to meet her by the Crowing Cock in the west end of the Docklands at eleven." He shook his head.

Diana looked at the clock. It was only nine. "Good." Then she stood. "I propose that Sin keeps his meeting."

Minnie crinkled her brow. "What do you mean? You mean he goes and claims he failed?"

"No, precisely the opposite."

Exile's insides dropped to his toes. "Absolutely not."

"What does she mean?" Daring asked crinkling his brow.

"We've got the carriage, the captor, and the captive," Diana said, spreading her hands along her dress. "All we're missing is the driver."

Daring scratched his temple. "But the driver would never help us."

Diana shrugged. "I think Vice could pass. He's the right height."

"Dear God, Diana, ye're no' actually thinking

what I think ye're thinking?" His insides turned with a sick dread.

"What's she thinking?" Daring demanded.

Exile stepped closer. His fingers itched to pull her close and never let her go. "She's going to use herself as bait."

Diana's own stomach clenched. She didn't love the plan, didn't even like it. But she couldn't think of another. How else was she going to get Anne back and capture, as Exile said, Lady Abernath?

Diana straightened her spine. She needed to do this. "I'd like to think of myself as more of a carrot. Draw her out."

Sin leaned forward. "And Anne? You'll keep her safe won't you? Bring her back?"

She looked over at Sin. "I'll do my best. And I mean that." She bent down. "Women need to protect little girls."

Exile pulled her back up to standing, his large hand gentle under her elbow. "Yer sisters and yer cousins, they'd protect ye no matter what."

She flushed. She knew what he was referring to. Her secret. The one she hadn't shared because it filled her with shame. She looked over at him, her heart beating wildly again. She did love him. She ached with it. And while he'd confessed his feelings for her, he hadn't made any sort of commitment. Diana didn't blame him but what she wanted to do tonight, this was her penance, she supposed.

"Of course we would," Minnie answered. "Which is why I want to go in Diana's place. She's been in enough danger for one night."

"No." Daring replied before Exile could. "Absolutely not."

"Besides." Diana reached over and touched a lock of Minnie's hair. "You'll never pass for me with that wild mane."

Minnie clucked her tongue. "Don't be silly. I'll wear a cloak."

But it was Exile who answered. "Diana will go." Then he turned to her. "But only if ye let me come too."

She could only nod, the words sticking in her throat. He did care about her and he understood her too. She suddenly didn't care about whether or not he proposed marriage. This man was everything to her.

"I ken ye're strong." He raised his hand to her lips, giving the back a light kiss. "But promise ye'll hide behind me if ye need to."

Her mouth opened and then closed. "I will."

Some of the tension relaxed out of her shoulders. Odd since she was about to go into the most dangerous situation in her life. But Callum knew her strengths, her weaknesses, her greatest secret. She could just be herself with him, and she loved who she was when he was around. "And Callum…"

"Yes?" he whispered.

"I love you, too." The future didn't matter to her in this moment. Her feelings were what was important.

Without another word, he leaned down and kissed her. Minnie gasped, but Callum paid her no mind.

It was a short kiss but somehow full of the emotion passing freely between them. Then he raised his head. She stared up into his eyes. "I can't believe you just did that."

"Believe it," he answered, cupping her cheek. "I'll take Sin's place. The only challenge is that she might spot either Vice or myself and then the jig is up."

Diana twisted her mouth. "Let's hope Bad and Vice can find the driver. His cloak would really come in handy."

"We didn't find him but we located a cloak exactly where Diana said it would be next to a pool of blood," Bad called from the terrace doors. "Lady Diana, remind me not to anger you."

Diana frowned at the cloth in Band's hand. Was that the cloak? She'd only seen it and the man for a second before she'd knocked him with the stick. It would have to do. "Well, we've got the cloak at least."

Daring cleared his throat.

Diana shivered and Callum pulled her closer. The man had a point. She'd just had everyone agree to a terribly dangerous plan. "I suppose I shouldn't change. I rather look like I've been kidnapped."

"I want to go too," Sin said from his seat on the bench.

"What?" Daring turned to him. "Out of the question."

"Please," he begged. "I swear on all that I hold dear that I will help you. I should have come to you to begin with instead of going along with Abernath's plan. I can pretend to take Diana to her and then she won't be as suspicious. Exile can be in the carriage too. I'll get my daughter and Exile can spring out and capture Abernath."

Vice curled his lip. "You've lied to your own flesh and blood and tried to hurt someone we care about."

Sin looked up at his cousin. "It's Anne. Vice, please. After my wife's death, she's all I have. If something happened to her…" his face crumpled.

"Why didn't you tell me?" Vice grabbed Sin by the shirt.

Sin swallowed his Adam's apple bobbing up and down. "I was afraid."

Diana, deep in her heart, believed him. "We've all made mistakes." Then she touched Callum's shoulder. "I think it's time we forgive ourselves, don't you?"

He gave a stiff nod. "I hope ye're right to trust him."

"I trust you," she answered, reaching up to touch his face. "You'll keep me safe."

He leaned down and whispered in her ear, "And ye are worth ten of those other debutantes. There isn't a finer woman in all of Britain."

Diana pressed her lips together. Those words filled her heart. Tomorrow, she'd worry about the future. Tonight, she'd put her faith in him.

CHAPTER FOURTEEN

Diana sat next to Callum in the carriage, Sin across from them. He stared out the window, idling rubbing the lump on his head. A wave of pride washed over her. Apparently, she'd hit him quite hard.

Callum's hand reached out and touched hers, his fingers lacing through her own. She rested her head on his shoulder and she closed her eyes. Inside, the knot of tension eased a bit. His touch making her draw in a deep breath.

"It's all right, lass. We're going to be fine," he murmured against the top of her head.

"I know we are," Diana said as she lifted her head. "We'll get her back, Sin."

The other man's face spasmed in pain. "If anything has happened to her…"

Diana cringed. She understood. "Lady Abernath needs her so I'm sure your little Anne is fine. Try not to worry."

He gave a tight nod. "Exile, you won't count on me to protect Diana, correct? My first objective is—"

"Diana can protect herself." Then he nodded toward the goose egg bump on Sin's head. "But ye go straight for yer daughter. Dinnae worry about us."

Diana looked at Callum. Now that Sin had revealed his interest in Diana was only to see his daughter safely returned, Callum was far kinder to the man. She supposed she couldn't blame Callum for being upset. If a woman started sniffing around him…. She sat straighter. Diana might pull out all her hair.

The streets outside grew louder as they entered the Docklands. People called loudly to one another as they made their way from ships to taverns or back again. Their progress slowed. "Remember," Sin said as he looked out the window. "I am going to demand that she give me Anne before I hand you over."

"I remember," Diana held out her wrists so that Sin could loosely tie them. She'd have Callum do it, but Sin's knots had already proven terrible. "Keep the ties loose so I can escape."

He shook his head a ghost of a smile touching his lips. "Not something we need worry about."

Callum crouched in a shadow. "Do you think she'll know Vice isn't her driver?"

Diana's stomach churned with apprehension when she considered all the possible events that could go wrong. "I'm more worried the driver found his way to her first."

Sin rubbed his head. "If he feels anything like me, he didn't."

Callum patted her hand. "Besides, Daring and Bad are just behind us. They'll sneak in to help too. Don't forget that."

The carriage rolled to a stop and Vice came to open the door. "I don't see her," he mumbled as he pulled the hat down lower.

Sin took her arm and pulled her cloak tighter about her shoulders. "She's just over there," he whispered, just low enough so that only they could hear. "She has Anne," his voice broke on the girl's name as he gave Diana a decided tug toward Lady Abernath.

Several other people milled about but Diana caught sight of the pale blonde hair hidden in the shadow. Next to her was a small girl, no more than five, looking frightened but unharmed. She tugged toward Sin the moment she saw him. "Daddy," she cried. Amazingly, Lady Abernath let the child go.

Sin pulled harder, reaching out his hand to the girl. But then, stopped.

The driver appeared next to Anne and grabbed her arm, pistol in hand. "What sort of funny business are you up to?" the man barked.

Sin stopped, his face going a shade of white, the pistol pointed at his daughter's head as the little girl began to cry. Diana's own knees weakened but Sin had frozen.

"Let me go or I'll smack you again," Diana called, pulling her arm from his grasp. He tightened his grip and looked at her. Her eyes widened as she attempted to wordlessly communicate her plan. "One egg wasn't good enough for you? I said let me go." Then she pulled again.

The other man's eyes widened. "Hit you too, did she?" His eyes travelled to the large egg on Sin's head. "For a woman, she'd good with a cane." The gun lowered. "We're gonna do this exchange nice and slow and then I'm going to give you your own lump." The man leered at Diana.

"Now, now." Lady Abernath stepped up next to him. "Diana is a strong woman and we admire her kind," Lady Abernath said as she gave her a slow smile.

Diana already knew what the countess wanted. She'd use that to her advantage now. "I personally admire you, my lady." She gave a curtsey. "And if you don't mind me saying so, I fancy myself a bit like you." Diana nibbled the inside of her cheek. Acceptance and praise. She said a silent prayer they would work.

"Do you?" The countess stepped closer. "Tell me how?" Her head cocked to the side. "You're not like the other women in your family. Which one married Effington? Lady Emily? She seems only weakened by her affection for that man."

Diana held her chin higher. Jack and Emily had had a rough start to be certain. Not that Diana didn't wish the best for them but she'd play their relationship to her advantage now. "I can't disagree. But Emily isn't known for her strength of character. I, however, am strong, as has been mentioned, smart enough, and yet still taken advantage of by the very men who should protect me." It was a gamble on Diana's part.

"Who took advantage of you?" Lady's Abernath's voice had dropped low.

Diana closed her eyes. She was going to reveal her secret in front of Sin but the child needed her. "My last suitor. He…" She licked her lips, "Took liberties that I—"

A hiss from Lady Abernath made her snap open her lids. "Pigs. All of them." Lady Abernath's hands trembled. "Even men who are supposed to be your family, your guardians, can use you like a cheap piece of trash."

Diana gave a tight nod, her stomach lurching. What had happened to this woman? She knew Lady Abernath had done terrible things, but in her heart, Diana knew horrible things had happened to the countess. "Exactly. We can help each other. There's no need for this." And she lifted her tied hands from the cloak. "If I help you, will you help me?"

Lady Abernath took two steps forward. "Yes, I—" Diana could see genuine relief in the woman's eyes. "I never wanted to hurt anyone. I just need the world to know I'm not a bad person. Bad things have happened to me and—" But then she stopped, her eyes travelling over Diana's shoulder. "Liar!" she yelled and then, "Fire the pistol!"

Exile had crept from the carriage, amazed that Diana seemed to have the situation in hand. No one had even asked who the new driver was. He held in a snort of contempt. Moving to the shadows, he crept along the wall of the building. Vice had slipped behind the carriage, also making himself unseen but close to the action.

He watched as Diana held up her tied hands,

lulling Abernath into trust, complacency. What was Diana's plan? Surely Exile was still going to try and capture the other woman? The driver made that harder with his presence but Vice was creeping along the building on the other side of the alley and he'd nearly reached the driver who had at least dropped the gun.

Skulking past them, Vice moved off the wall to step just behind the other man. Vice nodded. It was time.

Exile stepped from the shadows and Abernath saw him the moment he did. "Liar! Fire!" she yelled.

Exile didn't think. Instead, he hurtled himself at Diana.

The driver raised the gun and with sickeningly slow motion, pulled the trigger, aiming the barrel directly at her chest. His heart ceased even beating while his body moved, grabbing her and spinning her as they fell so he blocked her body with his own.

He felt the bullet tear through his coat and shirt, then a burning pain as it split his flesh on the outside of his arm. But the pain was of little consequence as he landed on his back, Diana tucked against his chest.

For a moment, he lay still, trying to decide how hurt he was before he came to his senses and rolled so that Diana was under him, tucked safely underneath his much larger body.

She tilted up her head, her eyes wild with fear. "Anne?"

Exile didn't want to look away, but reluctantly, he tore his gaze from hers. Vice had the driver on the ground, Sin had his child in his arms and Lady Abernath was gone.

Exile let out a groan. "Damn it all to hell."

"What is it," Diana asked pushing against his chest.

"We lost her again." He ground out between clenched teeth.

Diana relaxed underneath him, her arms circling around his neck. "But we're all safe, right?"

"Right," he answered dropping his nose to hers. "Are you hurt anywhere?"

"What the bloody hell happened?" Daring said from just above them.

"The driver tried to kill Diana," Sin said even as he clutched his daughter to his chest. "Vice, did you get the weapon?"

"I did," Vice called from his right. "And this guy isn't waking up anytime soon. When he does, it will be from inside a ccll."

He didn't bother to look up, sure Vice had everything under control. Instead he focused on the woman underneath him. "Diana, are ye all right?"

She nodded. "I'm fine. Thanks to you." One of her hands slid into his hair. "You know how I keep saying that I don't need anyone?"

"Yes," he answered, his voice rougher than usual.

"I lied," she whispered. "I needed you tonight. I need you still."

"I need ye too," he answered and then he leaned down and kissed her.

CHAPTER FIFTEEN

DIANA NEVER WANTED to be anywhere else in her life but snug against this man. As his lips pressed to hers, the rightness of their kiss settled over her like a warm blanket. Or perhaps that was his furnace of a body managing to heat her despite the cold ground under her back.

He lifted his head. "Leave yer window unlocked tonight."

"What?" she asked, but he was already rising, pulling her up with him, her body tingled at the idea that'd he'd visit her this evening. At some point this evening, she'd decided that she didn't care about the future. She wanted this man now.

"Christ, Exile," Bad said as he approached the group. "I've missed all the action and you're bleeding."

Diana started, then began a frantic search of Callum.

Daring stood, his eyes travelling up and down them both. "We heard the shot. I repeat, why didn't you wait?"

"Lady Abernath was about to complete the exchange…" Vice started.

"I had her under control," Diana answered, only half listening. She found the spot on his arm where the blood was staining his sleeve. "Take off your coat."

"I'm fine," Callum gave her an easy smile as he stroked her cheek. "It's barely a flesh wound."

"Take it off," she insisted as she tugged at the lapels pulling the fabric down his shoulders.

"Honestly, Sin got it far worse when I split him with my blade." He shrugged off the coat to show her the small tear in his shirt. She pulled the rip wider to see that he truly had a tiny wound on his arm.

Sin, carrying his daughter, came to inspect the wound. "He's right."

Daring snapped open the carriage door. "Vice, you drive Exile, Diana, Sin, and the child to my house. Bad and I will take our friend here to the Bow Street Runners. Then we need to discuss how we plan on protecting the Chase women. This is twice that Abernath has entered someone's home and staged an abduction."

Everyone nodded and Callum wrapped an arm about her waist, pulling her tight to his side. "I won't let anything happen to ye."

Diana believed him. Strong as she was, she'd let her guard down with this man and he cared for her anyway. "I know." She gave him a soft smile. "Thank you."

"The steps we've taken aren't nearly enough. It's time to get far more serious." Daring scrubbed his face.

Exile nodded and then helped her into the carriage and as he sat, she snuggled into his side. She'd never wanted a man to protect her before. But now that she had him, she wasn't sure she wanted to let him go. That made her pull back. Callum had never promised a future. In fact, he'd been adamant that he couldn't marry her.

Unlike Charles, he'd never made her false promises. And what she did next was her choice. But she already knew what she wanted to do. She'd be his, even if that was for just one night.

Exile helped Diana out of the carriage and into

Daring's home. Tomorrow, he would propose, in front of Diana's parents. Tomorrow, he'd read Fiona's letter and respond inviting her to London to participate in a season. With the help of his friends, he'd surely find her a suitable match.

But tonight, after what had happened, he had no intention of leaving Diana alone.

Tucking her under his arm, they entered the house, Sin just behind him with his daughter. Minnie stood waiting, her hands clasped together as she nibbled her lip. Next to her, Jack stood with his arm about Emily.

Minnie cried out as she saw them, rushing to hug her cousin. Reluctantly, Exile let her go.

Assessing Sin, the usually handsome man seemed haggard as he held the sleeping child in his arms. "You should stay here. Go to bed."

Sin gave him a look of surprise. "I thought for sure you'd want to murder me after all this."

Exile shrugged. "If it had been my child…" He wanted to express that he understood. "Ye'll be safer here anyhow. I'll convince Vice and Bad to stay and there will be multiple men here in case anything should arise."

"I think it's a fine idea," Diana added. "Minnie, you wouldn't mind if Sin stayed?"

"Heavens no." She reached for Sin's arm. "Let's

get you upstairs and tucked into a room. Emily, write to our parents telling them that Diana is staying again. Tell them the party is going very well and we'll be too late for her to return home."

Emily nodded. "Of course." Then she looked to Diana. "I feel responsible. I—"

"You aren't." Diana gave her a smile. "Don't even think it."

"Jack." Minnie turned to Emily's husband. "Start assembling the staff, I'll need to speak with them about the guests." Then Minnie turned back to Exile. "I trust you'll keep Diana safe while I'm gone."

"Ye have my word," he answered, pulling her close again.

The moment that Minnie disappeared, Exile started up the stairs, looking for a quieter sitting room. "Why did Minnie just leave us alone?" Diana asked as they entered a lovely room.

Exile sat, pulling her into his lap. "She kens that tonight the normal rules dinnae apply."

Her nose brushed his and a tingling shot straight to his groin from just the light touch. "They don't?"

"No." He grimaced, a look of exaggerated pain. "I was shot while protecting ye."

She leaned back, looking down at him, her lips pressed tighter. But she couldn't quite hide her smile. "A tiny wound if ever I saw one."

He stroked her cheek. "Ye told Lady Abernath yer secret. She can use it as a weapon against ye."

Diana shrugged. "Funny thing. I don't care what she does with the information. I guess I never did. I believed I wasn't worthy of anyone's love because of what I'd done. It was always about me."

Exile shook his head. "How can ye be so damned intelligent?"

She dropped her nose to his again. "Let me tell you, if I am so smart, that you aren't responsible for your cousin's death."

He pressed his forehead to hers. "Saving ye tonight, in some strange way, makes me feel better. Like I lived when he died to do some good in this world. All this time, I felt like he should be alive and I should be dead because he deserved it more."

Diana took several ragged breaths. "You're a fine man, Callum. I wouldn't love you if you weren't. Stop trying to live the life he would have chosen and follow your own destiny."

He stopped and looked deep into her eyes. The words were so simple, but they rang with a truth that took his breath away. This whole time he'd been so focused on how Ewan would have been Earl, who Ewan would have cared for and helped. "I…"

"Everything all right?" Minnie asked, entering the room. She didn't even blink at the fact Diana was in his lap when she sat across from them. "I didn't want to ask before, but what happened tonight?"

Exile listened as Diana relayed the events of the evening, Minnie gasping a number of times. "So Lady Abernath is still at large?"

Diana nodded. "And Grace and Ada are in even more danger than we imagined. Abernath isn't just bad, she's unhinged."

Minnie nodded. "We have to tell our parents the full extent of what's happened. If we don't…"

"I know." Diana looked in Callum's eyes, her own scrunched in pain.

He stroked her cheek. "Ye should go to bed. It's been a trying evening."

Bed? Sleep was the last thing she wanted but then he raised his brows giving her a side stare. Suddenly Diana realized he wasn't actually discussing sleep. "You're right. I am exhausted."

Emily walked back in the room. "Exhausted? Don't go to bed yet. I was so worried and I've hardly even seen you."

Diana sighed. Her sister was right. She'd been so wrapped up in the situation with Lady Abernath and, honestly, her feelings for Callum, that she'd barely seen her sister since she'd returned from her elopement. "How are you feeling?"

Emily shrugged. "Good overall. A little tired and a bit nauseous." She touched her belly.

Diana glanced at Emily's belly too. Her sister was pregnant. Soon she'd have a baby of her very own. Why did that sound so wonderful? She'd never considered that. If she didn't marry, she wouldn't have a child. Well, she supposed she could. Her gaze strayed to the man who had just slid her from his lap and tucked her into his side.

Then she thought of Harry. Not that she would ever be the horrible mother Lady Abernath had been, but still. The child's future was unknown. She nibbled her lip.

"How do you think Malice and Cordelia did, taking a child with them on their honeymoon?"

Emily shrugged. "They were going to visit Malice's family." Her hand held her chin. "But why did they take responsibility for Lady Abernath's child again?"

Diana's gut clenched. She'd likely made a mistake. "Well, he didn't have anyone else."

Emily looked to Minnie. "Are they taking him to family then? I know why he can't go back to the countess, but why is Cordelia responsible for someone else's child?"

Minnie shrugged. "I think Harry reminded Malice of himself."

Emily nodded absently. "How old was the boy?"

Exile squeezed her waist. "I can't recall."

But Jack chose that moment to walk back into the room.

"Jack," Emily called. "How old is Harry?"

Jack stopped, turning pale.

"I think he was four," Minnie said, and then she too sat up. "Which would mean…"

The room filled with a breathless silence and Diana didn't dare move. Emily turned to her husband. "Why didn't you tell me?"

Minnie had both her hands over her mouth.

Jack took a single step toward her, his hands up. "He doesn't look anything like me, or Daring, he…"

But Minnie let out a gasp as she stood.

Emily stood too, her eyes welling with tears. "You lied again when you promised you wouldn't."

"I didn't lie, I—"

"Get out," Emily said, pointing at the door. "I don't want to see you ever again."

"Emily," Diana started, reaching for her sister.

"Stay out of it," Emily barked, sounding far more like Diana might.

Diana snapped her lips closed. She didn't blame Jack for not sharing. But Emily's trust in her husband had been hanging by a thread.

Jack took another step toward her. "Please. Love. I had no idea until a few days ago and…"

"A few days?" Her voice rose with every word. "You've known for a few days and you didn't tell me?"

"I don't know anything," he answered, trying to shuffle even closer, but Emily planted both hands on his chest and pushed him backward.

"What's wrong?" Daring said as he walked in with Bad behind him. Vice had already kicked up his feet as though he'd bought a ticket to the theatre.

"You." Minnie pointed an accusing finger at her husband. "You lying piece of dung. I'm going to have your—"

"What the bloody hell?" Daring stalked over to his wife. "Minnie, what's happened that you're so angry—"

Minnie brought her hand down across her husband's cheek. "How could you not tell me?"

Daring held his face, but red skin peeked out from under his hand.

"They know about Harry," Jack said quietly.

"The four of us need to talk." Daring reached for his wife's arm and began pulling her toward the door.

Jack tried to do the same to Emily but she ripped her arm from his grasp. "I'm not talking to you about anything ever again." Without warning, he swept an arm under her knees and picked her up.

As the two couples left, Bad and Vice jumped up to follow. "Let's listen at the door," Vice said in a loud whisper.

"Good idea," Bad answered, slapping the other man on the back. "This is better than the club."

Diana started to rise to follow too. She was worried about Minnie and Emily, but Callum's hand held her in place. "They'll be fine. The child isnae Daring's or Jack's. Minnie and Emily will see that in time."

"What shall we do, then?" Diana asked, turning to look at him. His eyes had darkened as he stared back.

"Well, considering I have a wound on my arm that's yet to be bandaged, I'd love yer aid and I didn't really fancy climbing through yer window anyhow."

Diana pressed her lips together. "I should say no."

He leaned closer, his breath tickling her ear. "I can't leave ye alone. No' tonight." He brushed his fingers down her cheek and over her neck. "I just want to make sure no one tries to hurt ye."

Her insides tingled. How could she say no to that?

CHAPTER SIXTEEN

Exile half carried Diana to her room, his body taut with anticipation. He didn't plan on making love to her. He just wanted to hold her in his arms, feel her heart against his, and know for certain that she was safe.

That was enough.

But then she leaned into his neck, placing a feather-light kiss against his rough skin and his breath halted in his chest, everything inside him tightening. Damn that felt good.

"Diana," he rumbled, squeezing her tighter. "That feels too good. Ye cannae--"

"Can't?" she whispered close to his ear, her breath sending tingles careening down his skin. "Why not?"

"I want to be a gentleman. I—"

She laughed then. A throaty little chuckle that

made his cock swell. "You're coming to stay in my room. How is that gentlemanly?"

"It isnae" he growled back. "But it could be."

Diana pointed toward the right. "That way." Then she tightened her hands around his neck. "So why was I going to leave my window open?"

"I…" He swallowed as she gestured to a door. Flinging it open, he stepped inside, then quickly closed the large wooden door and locked them in. "I want to feel yer heartbeat against mine. Feel yer breath and ken ye're safe."

She stilled, except her hands, which slid to his cheeks. "That is the sweetest thing anyone has ever said to me."

Without thinking, he dropped his mouth to hers, giving her a kiss meant to be a promise but somehow, the touch grew and intensified until they were both panting for breath.

"What did ye think tonight would be?" he finally raised his head to ask.

Her eyes were half open and her lips pouty and swollen as she stared back. "I thought you would make love to me."

He groaned and kissed her again. Damn, he wanted to. More than he could say. But tonight was not the night. First, he didn't have to ask to know that his rescue had softened her. Made her more receptive. And he could justify making love to her because he had every intention of marrying her. But, the man he wanted to be would not take advantage. And honestly, he didn't want to elope like Jack and Emily, because Diana wound up pregnant. Their wedding would be in a church with her entire family in attendance. If he were going to alienate the only family he had left, he would not push away hers too. "I would like nothing more."

She quirked a brow as she rose up on tiptoe to kiss him again. Without thought, he squeezed her waist tighter, pulling her body against his. When she slid back down on her heels, her voice was playful. "Then I suppose we don't have a problem."

He cleared his throat. "Just one." Sliding his hands up her back, he felt the large rip in her dress. There was no saving the garment. Rather than undo each button, he gave a tug, the bodice giving way and falling open. "I won't leave ye with a child out of wedlock."

Her mouth tightened. "That had occurred to me too. I will miss having a baby of my own."

Exile scrunched his brow as he worked the sleeves off her arms. "I think we'll have plenty of children."

Diana shimmied the gown down over her hips.

"How do you figure that? Didn't you just say you didn't want to impregnate me?"

"Tonight," he answered. "Once we're married, I'll spend endless hours accomplishing the task."

"Married?" Diana, now in her corset and chemise took a step back. "Did you say married?"

"Yes," he held her face. "Is that a problem?"

"Problem?" Diana couldn't think the words let alone speak them. "Is marrying you a problem?"

Exile squinted at her, cocking his head to the side. "Ye're right. That was a lousy way to ask." Then he dropped down to one knee, reaching for her hand.

Her heart thudded in her chest so loudly, she could hardly hear. "Diana Chase, would ye do me the honor of becoming my wife?"

"I'm dressed only in a corset and chemise," she whispered back, her hand covering her chest.

He grimaced. "I ken I wish I'd asked ye when ye were sitting in the garden out on the terrace of a fancy ball."

She shook her head. "I don't care about traditions."

He gave her a soft smile. "That's one of the things I love about ye."

"I just didn't expect you to ask. I thought this would just be for tonight. I—"

"Are ye complaining?" he asked.

She shook her head, too overwhelmed to answer right away. "No," she squeaked.

"Are ye going to say yes?" He stood, clasping her other hand.

"Yes," she answered again.

He gave her hands a firm squeeze. "Tomorrow I'll ask again in front of yer family. But I wanted ye to understand tonight what I am thinking."

Her mind began to work again. Part of her was tempted to ask what had changed. Why he hadn't wanted to marry her to begin with but she didn't want to ruin this perfect moment. And so, rather than ask, she stepped closer, her chest just touching his, their hands still laced together. "Yes, I'll marry you."

"Good," he answered and then he kissed her again.

This kiss set fire to her blood and made her ache in places she didn't even know existed as his mouth took hers over and over. She barely noticed as the strings of her half corset gave way and the garment fell to the ground.

Not breaking their kiss, she tugged at the ties of his shirt, yanking the garment free. When he winced, she finally broke their kiss. "I forgot about your arm. I am so sorry."

"No' to worry, love," he answered, pulling the cloth up over his head. Then with his uninjured arm, he lifted her off the ground and carried her over to the bed.

She ran her fingers through his hair, loving the copper that glinted from the strands. One candle burned next to the bed, its light catching the flecks of red.

He lay her down on the mattress, then grabbed the hem of her chemise to skim the fabric up her thighs even as his lips kissed a path down. Diana wiggled out of garment and sent it sailing onto the floor as she lay in nothing but her stockings before him.

"Diana," his voice was hoarse as he trailed a hand down her body. He cupped one breast, then the other, lightly tweaking her nipples in a way that made her gasp and arch for more. "Ye're so lovely. It almost hurts..." He trailed off, dropping his mouth to one breast.

A moan ripped from her lips as he sucked in the sensitive flesh, causing it to peak.

But he didn't stop there. Lower and lower he

kissed, raising shivers and sighs of delight to fall from her lips until he dropped his mouth to her most intimate parts. Then no sound came out at all as her body spasmed in pleasure.

But he didn't stop with just one touch, over and over, he ran his tongue along her flesh, causing pleasure to build inside her until she thought she might burst from it.

She'd been with a man, she knew that. But the experience had been nothing like this. Callum was everything to her. She could think of nothing else as her body fell over the edge, crashing into an abyss of pleasure.

CHAPTER SEVENTEEN

EXILE WANTED to roar his own satisfaction as he listened to her moans of pleasure. Giving had never been so satisfying. He meant to keep his promise. He'd not risk impregnating her tonight, but giving her pleasure like that was all the satisfaction he'd need. He'd remember this night for the rest of his life.

His boots and pants were still on and he sat up to take the damned things off. He'd like to hold her close. He was certain she'd fall instantly asleep after what she'd just experienced, but instead she slid to the floor, still clad in nothing but stockings. "Was that your solution for making love to me without actually making love?"

"It was." He grinned as she slid off one of his hessians. "Diana." He looked down at her dark hair and eyes as she looked up at him. "Diana, I love ye so much."

"I love you, too," she answered sliding off the other boot. "Now lay back."

"Why?" he asked, tensing a bit. What was she going to do? But as her hands slid up his thighs, he began to understand. "Diana."

"Have you done this before? Does it work for you the way it did for me?"

His mouth went dry. "It works," he hissed.

She began undoing the complicated falls of his trousers. "Can you teach me?"

His cock already straining, he nearly exploded. "I have a feeling ye'll know what to do."

Sure enough, the moment she'd pulled his trousers down one of her delicate hands wrapped around his staff. His head fell back as his vision blurred. "Feck," he moaned.

She gave a small tug, making his body clench. "Do you like that?"

"Yes," he hissed as she moved her hand. Then, sweet Jesus above, she dropped those petal-soft lips to the head of his manhood, raining kisses upon it until she slid him into her mouth.

He nearly died of pleasure as he twisted his hand into the silky strands of her hair. She responded by taking more of him into her mouth.

His throat went dry as she slid back up his shaft. "If you weren't so large, I could take more of you—"

His free hand stroked her cheek. "That's perfect. Do it again."

She did, over and over, taking him into her mouth until he couldn't think, barely breathe. Reaching down, he pulled his staff from her mouth as he convulsed in pleasure. Diana nibbled her lip as she looked up at him. "Why did you pull it out of my mouth?"

He blinked back, barely able to string a thought together. "The seed. It doesn't taste…" The words died as she leaned down and licked his stomach.

"I like it."

Dear Lord. He was never letting this woman go.

She slid up his body, curling into his side. "You were right. I am exhausted."

Grabbing the blankets, he covered them up. "Then let's sleep. We've a big day tomorrow."

She burrowed in deeper to him. "We do." Then she let out a sigh. "But even if this was just tonight. It was perfect, Callum. Thank you."

He didn't respond as he looked over at her. Did that mean something? Surely, she was just saying thanks. But he wrapped her tighter in his arms. Somehow, he had that unsettled feeling that something was about to go wrong.

Diana woke the next morning in bed alone. She sat up, pulling the covers about her, as she nibbled her lip. Where was Callum? Searching about, she noticed a slip of paper on her pillow.

Diana,

I'll see you at half past three. I've sent a formal invitation to your parents. Don't be late, my love.

Callum

She read the note again. Why did he leave? Why didn't he tell her why he'd left? Then she remembered. She was at the duke's home. He likely hadn't wanted to get caught. But then why not wake her?

She climbed from the bed and slipped her chemise back on, ringing for a bath. She tried not to let her thoughts run away with her.

She'd only expected one night. Granted, he had proposed, but she was not going to start doing that girly thing where she second-guessed every decision she'd made.

Still, as she soaked in the tub, doubts plagued her.

What if he'd changed his mind about the marriage? What if he'd lied about his intentions all together? Charles had.

But then she forced herself to stop.

Whatever else she knew, Callum had real feelings for her. He'd saved her from a bullet, for pity's sake.

She drew in a deep breath. It was time to stop hiding. That wasn't who she was. Funny, she'd never realized that she used her own strength as a shield.

Climbing from the bath, she dressed and made her way downstairs to breakfast.

Minnie sat at the table alone. "What are you doing here?" she asked, sliding into the seat next to her cousin. "Married women dine in bed."

"Not today they don't." Minnie looked out the window, her eyes puffy. "I couldn't be in my room any longer."

"Minnie." She reached for her cousin's hand.

Minnie clasped Diana's fingers. "I know Harry isn't his and if he were, I'd take the boy in. It's the secret that hurts."

Diana nodded. "I understand. But try to see it from his perspective. If he was fairly certain that Harry wasn't his, why upset you?"

"Is that how we're viewing it?" Emily asked as she walked in and sat next to her sister. Then she dropped her head in her hands. "I've made a terrible mistake marrying Jack, haven't I?"

Diana drew in a breath. "I don't think so."

Emily lifted her head. "Truly? You've witnessed the last month, haven't you?"

Diana reached her other hand out to Emily. "He loves you and you love him."

Emily shook her head. "I was so wanton. Allowing him liberties. That caused our elopement, aided this mess with Lady Abernath. Exposed secrets and lies…"

Diana's mouth twisted. What if she had just made the same mistake by letting her desire for Exile cloud her judgment? "We are all weak sometimes."

"Not you," Minnie shook her head. "Diana, you are our rock."

Her insides quaked. "I shouldn't be. I've been wanton too. And not with a man who intended to marry me."

Emily sucked in her breath. "Exile?"

Diana shook her head, her chin tucking into her chest as her hands shook. "No. Before that."

"Wait," Minnie asked. "Before what?"

A flush of heat rose up Diana's face. "Never mind." She wasn't sure she could bear the shame.

Emily began rhythmically patting her hand. "What happened, Diana?"

She swallowed down the lump that had clogged her throat. "I gave my maidenhood to Charles."

"Oh, Diana," Minnie moaned softly. "You poor thing."

Emily wrapped her arms about her. "I'm so sorry. Why didn't you tell us? You must have been so frightened."

A silly tear threatened to run down her cheek. "You had your own worries and I…I was ashamed. I thought it made me less of a person."

"It doesn't," Emily insisted. "Don't ever think that."

Diana nodded. "Can I just say that Jack and Tag's mistakes don't make them less either."

Emily let go of her neck while Minnie squeezed her fingers all the harder. "I know you're right. But I'm still angry."

Emily dipped her chin. "I'm not certain in my case you are correct. I've caught Jack in a few lies now and—"

Diana held up her hand. "All the lies begin with his relationship with Lady Abernath and it's because he's ashamed. Trust me. It's something I understand."

"What about the club? He lied about that?" Emily sat straighter.

Diana patted her sister's hand. "Because Lady Abernath left him with a monstrous debt that he was trying to repay to marry you."

Emily chewed her lip. "Even if you're right, he should spend some time thinking about what he's done."

Diana looked at Minnie, who was smiling softly too. "Make sure he grovels when you do forgive him."

"Same to you," Emily whispered as Daring appeared in the door. His face was ashen and his hair a mess.

Minnie stood. "I'm still angry."

"I know." His eyes travelled to Diana. "But I am hoping we can make amends before half past three today?"

Minnie crossed her arms over her chest. "That's being rather specific."

Diana's heart jumped in her chest. "He invited you."

"What?" Emily asked. "What did he invite whom to?"

Daring lifted a piece of paper he was holding in his hand. "Exile is proposing to Diana today and we're all invited."

He hadn't been lying after all. Her eyes drifted closed. Half past three could not arrive soon enough.

CHAPTER EIGHTEEN

EXILE LOOKED at the clock for the fourth time in the past two minutes. It was still half past three. Why hadn't they arrived yet?

Then he shook his head. Because they'd arrive fashionably late and not on time.

He stood then, intent upon doing something to pass the time when the butler appeared in the doorway. "My lord, a lady is here to see you."

Diana. "Send her in," he said, clasping his hands behind his back. He'd left in the wee hours of the morning, not wanting to be caught. But he'd missed her all day.

The door creaked as it opened wider and Exile spun about. Diana did not stand in the door and for a moment, his brow crinkled in confusion. A red-haired woman stood in front of him, her brown eyes wide and her lip trembled as she stared back. "Lord Exmouth?"

"Yes?" he answered, not sure what to do.

"Pleased to meet ye," she gave a quick curtsey.

He bowed. "And ye as well. May I ask who ye are, precisely."

She worked her fingers along the edge of her satchel. "I've waited a verra long time to meet ye, ye see, and now that I am here, I am not quite sure what to say."

His insides began to twist into knots as dread made his limbs heavy. "Yer name?"

She shook her head. "I'm three and twenty now. All my friends have married."

The butler appeared behind her. "My lord, I've shown your other guests to the sitting room just down the hall."

"Other guests?" the woman asked. "Are ye having a party?"

"Not precisely," he said, then his chest squeezed tight. Diana appeared just behind the butler.

She caught Exile's eye. "I know I'm supposed to wait with the others, but I wanted to see you before…oh!" She caught sight of the lady, "I'm interrupting. My apologies." Diana gave a large smile. "Is this a relation of yours?"

His tongue tied in his mouth and he could say

not a word as the other woman turned to Diana.

"I'm Fiona MacFarland. His fiancée."

Diana's face went pale as a sheet as her eyes flew to his. Her mouth opened and then closed again. "I… I see."

Fiona turned back to him. "I came here to tell ye in person that yer aunt has passed away. She had a disease of the lung over the winter from which she never recovered."

Callum shook his head. His aunt is gone? "I didnae ken."

"My fault," Fiona said. "I couldn't tell ye in a letter."

Diana stared at them both, visibly shaking. He wanted to go to her but he wasn't sure he should. Fiona stole his attention again.

"I didnae ken how to write to the man who hadn't bothered to meet me in the three years we'd been promised to one another that his relation had passed," she said.

"Never met," Diana whispered. He wouldn't have heard her at all but he could see her lips moving.

"I'm sorry. Fiona." Then he looked at Diana. "Diana, ye dinnae look well. Come here."

"I don't think so," she answered, spinning around and leaving the room.

He started after her, but as he reached the doorway, Fiona grabbed his arm. "I never wanted to marry ye."

He stopped. "I didnae want to marry ye either."

She nodded. "That does make this easier."

"What's that?" His eyes crinkled at the corners as he tried to keep up.

She notched her chin. "I wanted to tell ye about yer aunt in person and say to ye that I've married another. With your aunt gone, I no longer feel responsible for fulfilling the match she set forth."

He blinked. "Wait. I thought I was marrying ye for yer benefit. She said…"

Fiona started then snapped her chin. "I don't need a man who loves England more than his home country."

Part of him wanted to laugh. This had all been a mistake. But another part looked down the hall to where Diana had disappeared. Would she ever forgive him?

DIANA HAD FOUND a door to the courtyard where she'd tossed herself on the ground and, for the first time in months, allowed herself to cry. They were tears that she'd held in for such a long time. Her worry over Charles, Emily's disappearance, her own fears from the last several days. But as she wept out all her worries, strong hands lifted her and silently settled her into his lap.

When she'd been wrung dry, she lifted her face, likely red and puffy beyond all recognition and said, "You're marrying her, aren't you?"

Callum looked softly down at her. "No, lass. If ye'll still have me, I'm marrying ye."

She shook her head. "But she's your fiancée."

"So are ye," he answered, raising his brows.

"How many can a man have?" she asked, but her point was ruined as she let out a loud hiccup.

"Just the one," he answered, smoothing back loose wisps of her hair. "Fiona and I have mutually agreed that a marriage between us was never a good idea."

"Is that why you didn't want to marry me before? Because of her?"

"Yes," he answered. "She was promised to Ewan when he died and my aunt felt I should honor the contract. I didnae even know her, Diana, and I certainly had no feelings for her beyond obligation. But my guilt over Ewan's death made it difficult for me to consider another option."

Diana gasped. "Oh. I see. I understand completely. You wanted to fill all his obligations and so you took up his bride as your own."

"Well," he grimaced. "I was dragging my feet. In five years, we never even met."

Diana reached for his face, holding his cheeks in her gloved hands. "I did catch that part, though no woman wants to meet her man's other woman." She gave him a long look.

"Diana," he answered, staring back. "Ye're all the woman I will ever be able to handle."

"Good," she answered, swiping at her face. "Because Bad was correct. You do not want to make me angry."

Callum laughed then, lifting her off the bench and into his arms. "Funny thing about ye, Diana. Ye may have the softest heart of all the Chases."

She shook her head. "You know. I just might."

"Now, let's get ye cleaned up. We've got an engagement to make public."

Diana shook her head. "My mother somehow knows already. Apparently, she was skeptical about allowing me to stay at Minnie's the past few days, but now she's convinced that Ada and Grace should also attend a dinner party thrown by Daring and Minnie. Thinks they'll leave with husbands."

Callum stopped, staring down at her. "Ye know. That isnae a bad plan."

Diana shook her head. "It's a dreadful plan. The worst."

He leaned down and kissed her cheek. "As long as ye're my wife, and yer family is all safe, I dinnae care how we go about it."

She gave him a large smile. "I agree. Except that Vice and Bad need to keep their hands to themselves. I've spent time with the two of them. They're the worst of the lot."

"That they are," he answered.

The door to the courtyard opened and Daring stepped out. "What the blazes is going on?" Daring yelled. "You've disappeared with an earl's daughter. Have you lost your mind?"

"No. We're coming," Callum called. "But we might need you to stall for a few more minutes."

"What has my life become?" Daring grouched as he turned back inside.

Callum leaned over. "Will you be at yer parents' tonight?"

She looked up at him. "I will."

"Is your window climbable?"

A little giggle escaped, her heart bursting with joy. "I'm on the second floor with a lovely trellis and balcony."

He leaned down. "Leave yer balcony door open tonight."

She caught her breath. "With pleasure."

CHAPTER NINETEEN

Diana stood by her open balcony door wearing nothing but a night rail. She'd shooed away her cousin and sister an hour prior, then had undone her hair. She wasn't certain if Callum still wanted to wait to be completely intimate until the wedding, but she knew that she did not want to wait another moment.

In fact, she might burst if he didn't arrive soon. Stepping out onto the balcony for the fourth time in as many minutes, she nearly screamed when a hand appeared on the railing.

Slapping her palms over her mouth, she stared as Callum's head appeared. "Ye were right. The trellis is exceptional."

She dropped her hands and stepped toward him as he pushed his upper body above the rail and then swung a leg over the side. "You came."

He stepped toward her, pulling her against his chest. "Of course I did. I cannae stay away from ye now that I ken we're to be married. The real problem is how we're no' going to get caught."

She slid her arms around his neck. "I've convinced my mother to have the ceremony in a fortnight. Perhaps one of my sisters will have a nice, long, proper engagement, but my father is so thrilled not to have to fund my season that I suspect they'll agree."

He grinned, capturing her lips. "Ye're not disappointed are ye? To be missing a large affair?"

"Goodness no," she answered, kissing him again. "The last emotion I feel is disappointment."

He slid his hands down over her back and then her behind, cupping the cheeks as he lifted her to press their hips together. Tingling sensations spread through her as his hard shaft pushed into her softness, making her weak with want.

Hoisting her up off the ground, he carried her back inside. "Diana," he said, his voice rough and low. "I want to wait but…"

"It's only a few weeks," she answered, as he sat on the bed with her in his lap, her legs on either side of his hips.

Callum grabbed her derriere again and pressing

her closer, they started to move together, even with their clothes still on, Diana thought she might die from need. A warm sensation coursed through her.

She fumbled with his shirt until she managed to pull it off his torso, then her hands were everywhere. She touched the hard strength of his shoulders, the muscled chest, flat stomach, and hard back, raking her fingers along the skin.

In answer, he lay back and began undoing the falls of his breeches. Then he had to sit up again, to wrestle them over his hips.

Diana lifted up to let him work and, in one quick movement, her night rail went sailing over her head.

He only managed to get his pants down to his knees before she pushed him back onto the bed and lowered herself onto his hard shaft.

Her eyes rolled back as he filled her insides in a way that was incredibly satisfying. Both because he felt so wonderful and because being with him like this made her feel worthy of love. "Oh, Callum," she breathed out, just holding him inside her.

He ran his hands over her front, touching every swell and angle. "Diana, my love," he murmured then he pulled her lower and as he slid out of her, took her lips in another heated kiss. "It doesn't get any better than this."

"No," she answered. "It doesn't." Then she slid back down him, drawing him into her body again.

The pace was slow but their caresses, their kisses, grew increasingly heated until the pace quickened, taking on a breathless quality that made Diana hot and hungry for more.

She held him tight as her body rode the sensation, drawing to the final climax where she screamed out his name.

She was still spasming inside when he rolled her over and thrust inside her two, three, four times before his own guttural cry joined with hers. She felt his warm seed inside her even as he held her close.

Diana stroked his hair, his warm weight on top of her as they lay still joined together. "I'll stay until just before dawn," he whispered.

"Wake me before you go," she answered, kissing him again.

"Soon enough, I won't have to go anywhere."

She smiled as he lifted her again and pulled back the covers. "I can't believe we're getting married."

"I can't believe it took me this long to decide." He kissed her again as he settled her into his arms. "I love ye, Diana."

"I love you, too," she answered as she rested her cheek on Callum's chest. She was home. There was no doubt about that. And as for her wedding, the day she'd never expected to have, she couldn't be more thrilled. It didn't matter to her where it was or what happened as long as she married her earl.

EPILOGUE

Two weeks later...

Diana stared down the aisle as Callum looked back, her heart ready to burst from her chest. Never had a man appeared more handsome than he did in this moment. He'd tied back his hair, his dark green eyes shining in the many candles lit in the church.

Her breath caught and she started for him, her father holding her back. "Steady, Diana."

She looked over to her father. "Is he not the most beautiful man you've ever seen?"

Her father wrinkled his nose. "I don't know about that, but I'm fairly certain, you are the most stunning bride that ever graced this church."

Diana looked down at the cream gown she'd

donned hoping to highlight her ivory skin and dark hair. "Thank you, Papa."

"Now let's get you married. I'm not certain what has filled the air but our girls have been struck by Cupid this spring."

Diana raised her eyebrows. Lady Abernath as Cupid? She wasn't sure she'd go that far, but despite everything that had happened, she still felt sympathy for the woman. And her actions had started an avalanche of marriages in the Chase family. "Now we just need to find husbands for Ada and Grace."

Her father gave her a small wink. "They're doing just fine."

Diana glanced toward the front of the church to see both Vice and Bad sitting on either side of the ladies. How did she tell her father that the two men had likely been ordered by their friends to sit there? "I'm not sure either of those men would make proper husbands…they're a bit…"

Her father held up his hand as the organ began to play. "We'll worry about them later. Right now, how about we focus on you?"

She smiled as they began to walk down the aisle. Sin was there with his lovely daughter and they waved. But Diana couldn't help but notice that Sin's gaze slid to her cousin, Mary. Mary, for her part, blushed a lovely shade of pink at the earl's gaze.

But she didn't have time to focus on anyone else as they reached the front of the church and Callum reached for her hand.

The moment his fingers touched hers, she relaxed, looking into his eyes, everything and everyone else melted away. "I love you, Callum Exmouth."

He gave her a soft smile. The sort that melted her insides. "I love ye, Diana Chase." He gave her fingers a light squeeze. "I never imagined there was a woman such as ye out there. I'd say ye were waiting for me but we ken ye don't wait for anything."

Laughter, reminded her they weren't alone. "It's a good thing too. You might be on your way to Scotland this very moment."

He pulled her closer. "That is very true and an excellent point. I don't want ye to mistake me. Ye are the perfect woman for me."

She let out a sigh as the priest moved forward. They were perfect together. Had been all along. And now they'd spend their lives together, filling each other in like the pieces to a puzzle. "And you are a wonderful man."

"Shall we begin?" the priest asked.

Callum nodded but Diana only smiled. Their story had begun the day they'd met in the club. This was only the next chapter.

VISCOUNT OF VICE

LORDS OF SCANDAL BOOK 4

Lord Blakely Everbee, The Viscount of Viceroy, sat next to Miss Ada Chase as they both watched her cousin walk down the aisle toward his friend, The Earl of Exmouth. He grimaced, inwardly, flexing his fingers. Vice bloody hated weddings. And he especially despised them while sitting next to an eligible woman who, if he wasn't mistaken, was going to cry.

He nearly spit as he spied the little drop of water forming in the corner of her eye. Then she did what all ladies did. With a delicate dab of her kerchief, she let out a soft sigh. The sort that might lull a man into going soft. "Isn't this just beautiful?"

Vice had to confess that while the wedding itself was dreadful, the sight of her wasn't terribly awful. It was rather nice, in fact.

He didn't dare credit her with any more than nice, however. He was considered by most to be exceptionally handsome, his features near angelic. And he held the women he dallied with to very high standards. They were the most beautiful, talented, gifted, or accomplished women in England and wider Europe for that manner. He'd had an affair, for example, with a gypsy known for her ability to read cards with deadly accuracy and drink vodka with the best men.

He'd carried on with the most famous actress in all of London, been with a Russian princess who was rich beyond his wildest imaginings. All in all, the list of women he'd shared a bed with was an accomplishment in and of itself. One he was proud of.

And Miss Ada wasn't list worthy. Yes, she was lovely with her pale auburn hair glimmering in the sun and her bright green eyes that only looked more sparkly with the sheen of tears. And yes, her figure was supple, the perfect amount of soft curves with an ample bosom and a tiny waist. Of course, her trembling lip as she stared at the bride and groom made him wonder what she might taste like. And the soft noise of satisfaction she emitted sounded like the sweetest pillow talk he'd ever heard. But Miss Chase wasn't accomplished at anything of significance…and therefore was not his sort at all.

"That kiss," she turned toward him then, her eyes a bit dreamy, her head tilted to one side. "Diana is glowing."

Vice's mouth twisted into a frown. "Glowing?" His mouth tasted like he'd eaten gravel.

Ada tapped his arm with her fan, a light tap that brushed against his waistcoat with a bit of a tickle. "Don't you see it? The color in her cheeks. Her breathless smile. It's just—"

"Beautiful?" Vice filled in the word she'd just used moments before. "You've already told us."

She turned toward him then, her mouth slightly parted. "You don't think so?"

He assessed her features. Her high cheekbones were flushed with a pinkish-brown hue that accentuated the tiny spattering of freckles across her nose. They were not to his usual taste at all, giving her an air of innocence, but he found he'd like to count them. Perhaps kiss a few. "Weddings are generally a bore. And even worse, all I can think is that the groom has given up all the fun in life to take care of a woman and a passel of brats that are soon to follow."

Ada sniffed, turning back toward the front. "My goodness, you are dreadful, aren't you?"

His best friend, the Baron of Baderness, sat two seats away, next to Ada's cousin, Lady Grace. Now

Grace was a woman that might make his list. The features of her face were a perfect mask of feminine beauty. Bad leaned over, making eye contact despite the two ladies between them. "He's beyond dreadful. I might use the word insufferable," Bad murmured just loud enough for the four of them to hear him.

Grace let out a tiny giggle. "You're quite funny. You're so quiet, I didn't realize." That made Bad snap his mouth shut and sit back in his chair.

It was Vice's turn to chuckle. "He isn't. He only makes a joke once every five years."

Ada's mouth curved into a small grin. The sort where her lips stayed together, not showing any of her teeth. But she shook her head, as though she disapproved, despite her relaxed features. Then one finger came to her chin. "Insufferable?" She looked back at him, her green eyes sparkling. "The word suits you."

He cocked a brow. By his estimation, Ada Chase had no right to give him any trouble at all. Six weeks prior, she, her sister, and cousins had entered into his secret gaming hell that he ran with five of his friends. They'd learned the men's secret and put themselves in danger. Now, he and Bad were being forced to babysit the only two Chase women who weren't wed. The job was worse than attending this wedding.

"And what word might suit you?" He returned, leaning closer. Which might have been a mistake. She smelled of cookies or cinnamon. Perhaps both. No wait, he caught subtle whiffs of honey laced into her sweet smell. Without meaning to, he drew in a deep whiff. Delightful.

She shrugged, but her face tensed and her hands clasped in her lap. Dropping her head to look down at her hands, she pursed her lips. "Am I to insert the word most often used to describe me?"

"If it pleases you." He sat back feeling as though he'd just won some unnamed battle of wits. He could see her discomfort.

Then she relaxed. Her head drew higher as the lines of her body straightened. Ada looked over at him then, leaning close. "My sister and cousins often call me *little bird*. I suppose it's because I do tend to flit with nervousness."

That sounded about right to him. Looking at her features now, she was just as beautiful, if not more so, than Grace. But she lacked the confidence that drew attention to those looks.

She pressed a bit closer still and her left breast brushed against his arm. His entire body clenched at the light touch as her breath whispered across the skin of his ear, near causing him to shiver. There was nothing mousy about that move. "But in the last year, I've gotten a new nickname."

He turned to her then, realizing just how close she was, an inch, perhaps two, and he could press his lips to her softly parted ones. He fisted his fingers to keep from touching her face. Damn, he wanted to kiss her. How was she doing this? "What is it?"

"Ruiner of rakes," she answered, looking him directly in the eye. "Can you imagine a sillier name?"

Was she moving closer? He blinked twice trying to make his eyes work properly when she straightened away again. "You? Ruiner of rakes? I've met some women in my day who could claim that title, but you? A woman capable of making a sinful man repent?"

She gave a tiny shrug. She didn't pull away but he did note a tiny crinkling about the eyes, almost as though she were wincing. "I know. It's absurd, really."

He narrowed his gaze. Was she challenging him? His mouth curved into a smile as a new idea caught his fancy. If she wanted to wage a war in the field of affection, he was game. And if she really did have a reputation as a reformer of rakes, well, she'd make a nice addition to his list.

Having her attention would help accomplish

another goal as well. In fact, his job would be far easier, if she wished to be by his side. He'd agreed to keep watch over her when she was in public. It was the very reason he sat next to her today. Ada had discovered a secret about his friends and he needed to make certain Ada kept that secret. And recent events dictated that he also keep her safe.

He gave her his most charming smile. "Not absurd at all. I see it now. Your hair reminds me of sunset on a warm summer day and your eyes are the color of new grass. How could a rake not be enchanted?"

Rather than smile, she grimaced, her sweet lips turning down into a decided frown. "I don't know what you're playing at, but it won't work with me."

He started, which pushed him toward the edge of his chair and his back slipped off the narrow strip of wood it had been leaning against. He was never clumsy and he didn't understand it now, but in sickening slow motion, he fell to the side, catching his hand on the very piece of wood that had just failed him. The problem was that his weight had shifted to one side of the seat, at least that was what he decided later. In the moment, however, he careened off to one side, both him and the chair crashing to the ground. Gasps filled the air as the organ came to a grinding halt. He looked up to find Ada staring at him as though he'd grown a second head.

Ada looked at the Viscount laying at her feet, tangled in his chair. She nibbled at her lip trying to decipher how bad the situation was.

First, she'd just lied through her teeth. No one in the history of the world had ever considered her a *ruiner of rakes*. It was a complete falsehood. In fact, they often teased her for being bland and frightened by everything, men especially.

Second, her lie had clearly discombobulated the Viscount and once he realized she'd fibbed, well he'd be even angrier. Ada never got away with falsehoods. Some people could, but not her. Diana swore that every lie was visible on her face. It must be true. How else did she get caught every time?

And she was certain he already suspected the lie. Hadn't he said so when he'd told her that he'd known women who could carry the title of rake-ruiner? She was certain he had. And implied in that statement were two facts she'd long known about herself. One, she was not that sort of woman at all. And two, a man like Viceroy would never be interested in her. He'd all but said the words himself.

"Lord Viceroy, are you all right?" She reached down as the entire wedding stopped to stare at them. He took her hand but was too tangled in the chair to get up.

Standing, she righted the wooden seat and then reached down for Lord Viceroy again. Wedged in a small aisle, she meant to help him stand with as much dignity as possible. But he pulled before Ada had planted her feet. Rather than helping him stand, she toppled forward landing directly on him, her face nearly smashing into his. He stuck his hand between them, which was a good thing. If he hadn't, their teeth might very well have crashed together but his knuckle hit her cheekbone and a sharp pain made her roll to the side. "Ouch," she cried.

He wrapped his other arm about her, just managing to keep her from crashing into the chairs while she planted one hand on the floor next Viceroy's face, the other pressing to his chest. Moving his hand, he cupped her cheek and turned her face. "Damn it all to hell," he muttered. "You're going to have a bruise."

She tried to scramble off his body, but her skirts were getting tangled from her movement on top of him. Her legs wound about his and their hips pressed together. All the contact…well…it was causing her to heat. Or was that her embarrassment?

No, it wasn't just that. She'd never touched a man like this before and he was so muscular underneath her. A pulse began to ache between her legs. So handsome...

Her breath caught and her eyes widened. Could he tell how she was responding? He was still studying her cheek. "Daring is going to kill me," he muttered under his breath.

"It's not your faul—"

As if he'd heard, Ada's brother-in-law, the Duke of Darlington, called from two rows back. "What is going on up there?"

Ada pressed her lips together. Daring, as Vice called Darlington, was her sister's husband. But he was also one of Vice's good friends and they owned a club together along with the Marquess of Malicorn, Earl of Exmouth, and the Baron of Baderness.

"It's fine," she called back as if that made everything all right. "We'll be up in just a moment. No need to worry."

"Bloody hell," he said, his normally pleasant features twisting into a frown. The man had blond hair with sky-blue eyes, chiseled features and full lips. Her breath caught again as her hand fisted in his shirt. Which only served to remind her how strong and hard his chest was.

Vice started to sit up and somehow managed to pull her up with him, climbing to his feet while holding her. He set Ada back on the floor, his hands firmly on her waist. "My apologies for falling. Thank you for attempting to help me. I did not intend to pull you…"

She waved her hand. "The fault was most assuredly mine." Then she took a step back, nearly tripping on Grace's feet.

Her parents had turned back to stare and Ada wished she could disappear into the floor. Everyone was staring. She wobbled and Vice's hands shot out to hold her in place again. Her skin shivered at his touch. He gave her another charming grin. The sort that looked practiced and false. Her shivers stopped. He made her weak in the knees but not when he looked so rehearsed. That look reminded her that she was one of many women, and likely the least of them.

"If you insist on taking the blame, I won't stop you." Then he winked.

Her eyes narrowed as she cocked her head to the side, assessing him. When they'd been tangled together on the floor, she'd forgotten what sort of man he was. For a moment, he was just the handsome, well-built man pressed against her. And honestly, she did respond to him in ways she didn't fully understand. But when he started talking…he made her angry, first and foremost. Most likely because she knew a man like him would never actually be interested in her. His stock lines were meant for any woman with a pulse. He didn't recognize her, of course, but Ada was well acquainted with Vice.

She knew what sort she'd marry. An affable fellow that her sister would likely call dull. Sure, Minnie and Diana had tamed rakes, but Ada, she'd be lucky to tame her red hair into a coif subdued enough for a merchant or a doctor. She'd been courted by an adventurer. Or that's what she liked to call him. A man who went off to exciting places to study animals. But even he'd left her. She just wasn't exciting enough, she was certain of it. "You do know that gentlemen take the blame as a rule."

"I'm no gentleman," he whispered leaning close. "But if you'd like me to, it can be all my fault. This time and every time."

Every time? What was that supposed to mean? She scrunched her brow but his wicked grin that curled his lips told her that he meant something untoward and was now making fun of her lack of experience.

There was no point in answering, so she sat down, staring straight ahead so as not to have to look at anyone. The wedding was over and the rosy feeling that had filled her chest watching the nuptials was gone. Which was all Vice's fault. Crossing her arms, she glared at him. She might hate that man.

Find Viscount of Vice on all major retailers!

ABOUT THE AUTHOR

Tammy Andresen lives with her husband and three children just outside of Boston, Massachusetts. She grew up on the Seacoast of Maine, where she spent countless days dreaming up stories in blueberry fields and among the scrub pines that line the coast. Her mother loved to spin a yarn and Tammy filled many hours listening to her mother retell the classics. It was inevitable that at the age of eighteen, she headed off to Simmons College, where she studied English literature and education. She never left Massachusetts but some of her heart still resides in Maine and her family visits often.

Find out more about Tammy:
http://www.tammyandresen.com/
https://www.facebook.com/authortammyandresen
https://twitter.com/TammyAndresen
https://www.pinterest.com/tammy_andresen/
https://plus.google.com/+TammyAndresen/

Read Tammy Andresen's other books:

Seeds of Love: Prequel to the Lily in Bloom series

Lily in Bloom

Midnight Magic

Keep up with all the latest news, sales, freebies, and releases by joining my newsletter!

www.tammyandresen.com

Hugs!

OTHER TITLES BY TAMMY

How to Reform a Rake

Don't Tell a Duke You Love Him

Meddle in a Marquess's Affairs

Never Trust an Errant Earl

Never Kiss an Earl at Midnight

Make a Viscount Beg

Wicked Lords of London

Earl of Sussex

My Duke's Seduction

My Duke's Deception

My Earl's Entrapment

My Duke's Desire

My Wicked Earl

Brethren of Stone

The Duke's Scottish Lass

Scottish Devil

Wicked Laird

Kilted Sin

Rogue Scot

The Fate of a Highland Rake

A Laird to Love

Christmastide with my Captain

My Enemy, My Earl

Heart of a Highlander

A Scot's Surrender

A Laird's Seduction

Taming the Duke's Heart

Taming a Duke's Reckless Heart

Taming a Duke's Wild Rose

Taming a Laird's Wild Lady

Taming a Rake into a Lord

Taming a Savage Gentleman

Taming a Rogue Earl

Fairfield Fairy Tales

Stealing a Lady's Heart

Hunting for a Lady's Heart

Entrapping a Lord's Love: Coming in February of 2018

American Historical Romance

Lily in Bloom

Midnight Magic

The Golden Rules of Love

Boxsets!!

Taming the Duke's Heart Books 1-3

American Brides

A Laird to Love

Wicked Lords of London

Printed in Great Britain
by Amazon